Haunted Pennsylvania
True Ghost Stories and Legends of the Keystone State
Written and Illustrated
by Jannette Quackenbush

Copyright © 2025 by Jannette Quackenbush

ISBN-13: 978-1-940087-77-1

Jannette Quackenbush is an author of over 50 books, folklorist, naturalist, and paranormal researcher. She focuses on ghost stories, folklore, and hiking trails in the Appalachian and southern U.S. Known for her engaging storytelling, she has published many works on local legends and haunted places. Her project, "Dark Journeys with Jannette," features guided hikes where participants explore haunted sites and learn about the region's folklore, connecting them to the rich cultural history and stories of the area. People always ask me, "Do you believe?" And here is how I feel, "Everybody is a skeptic until they experience something out of the norm. Then, all of a sudden, they realize there is more out there to discover, and they become part of this big community of others whose eyes are open to the unknown. And they want to know more, see more, adventure more. Do I believe? Well, I'd certainly rather be racing out to be with the believers, the adventurous ones who get out and explore. You can be among this community too—just get out there!"

The Ghost in the Parlor
(Adams County)

Baltimore Street—Gettysburg

The Moon Before the Storm

The people of Gettysburg didn't sleep well that summer. June's end brought hard rain and a swollen moon, and with it came stories—Rebels had crossed the Potomac.

They were in Chambersburg.

Then Carlisle.

Then Harrisburg.

By June 26, 1863 Confederate infantry filled Gettysburg's streets. Their boots were slick with horse dung and rainwater. The soldiers—hollow-eyed and hungry—forced open shop doors, ripped sacks of flour from wagons, and pulled whiskey bottles straight from under store counters. Townsfolk fled. But some stayed behind either by duty or by fate.

One was a seamstress named Jennie Wade.

She was twenty, small and dark-haired, tending to a neighbor's child and her youngest brother while her mother helped her sister Georgia recover from childbirth just blocks away.

The houses were close together. But death was closer.

Georgia's House

Jennie arrived at her sister's brick home on Baltimore Street just as the real battle began—July 1. The house was just two doors from the open countryside, near the graveyard. It should've felt safe.

It didn't.

Confederate sharpshooters took up positions in the tannery across the way. Union soldiers were crouched behind the McClellan garden fence, rifles ready. Men screamed behind the house. Some didn't stop.

The family moved Georgia's bed to the parlor. Her baby was just days old, and she couldn't walk far. Jennie stayed nearby, pumping water, tearing strips for bandages, and baking bread for the Union boys who pounded on the door at all hours. When they knocked, she handed it through the cracks. The house was already riddled with bullet holes.

Then came the shell.

Ten pounds of iron screamed in from the north, shot from nearly two miles away. It cracked through the shingles, snapped the ceiling boards, and embedded itself in the parlor wall.

It didn't explode. But it broke something in Jennie.

She fainted where she stood.

The Shot

At dawn on July 3, Jennie woke and prepared dough. Flour still dusted the shelves from the day before. Her mother lit the stove, ignoring the gunfire creeping closer. Jennie paused her devotions to speak a single line:

"If anyone in this house is to die today, I hope it is me—Georgia has that little baby."

The air was thick with smoke. The tiny house had no place to hide. And every window had a view to death.

Sometime just after 8:00 a.m., a Confederate musket cracked down the street. Some said the sniper mistook her for a soldier—dark dress, upright posture, and silhouette against the windowlight.

The bullet punched through the front door, passed through another, and struck Jennie in the left shoulder blade. It tore through her chest, shattered her heart, and lodged in her corset bones.

She dropped onto the parlor floor with the dough still on her hands.

Her skirt brushed against her mother's, and Mary Ann Wade said only one thing:

"Georgia, your sister is dead."

After

They laid Jennie's body in the cellar, on a bench beside the coal bin. For eighteen hours, the house shook with cannon fire. Soldiers crawled in and out, whispering to each other in gasps and curses.

The family did not bury her until nightfall.

They couldn't.

When they did, it was a shallow grave in the garden.

She was still dusted in flour.

A Letter That Never Came

A week before she died, her sweetheart—Jack Skelly—was shot and captured in Winchester. Before he was taken, he gave a letter to a Confederate soldier: Wesley Culp, a friend from Gettysburg, now fighting for the South.

Wesley promised to deliver it to Jennie.

He never did.

He died just outside town, killed in a skirmish while crossing back over farmland he once played in. Jack died in a hospital a few days later, never knowing Jennie was gone. His grave lies not far from hers.

The letter never reached her hand.

The Parlor

Today, the McClellan house still stands. It is quiet. Too quiet. Visitors report the smell of baking bread when no one is cooking. Others feel a cold pass through them like water, or hear footsteps near the parlor, just before 8:30 a.m. Some see a pale figure in the kitchen window.

She never left that house. And never will.

The General and His Dog
(Adams County)

Joseph Hummelbaugh Farmhouse—Gettysburg
The Wig Incident

Before blood soaked the fields of Gettysburg, before his name was cursed in whispers near the Hummelbaugh farmhouse, William Barksdale was mostly known for one thing: his wig.

It was 1858. Congress was a powder keg. On February 5th, fists flew between pro-slavery and anti-slavery legislators.

In the chaos, Representative Cadwallader Washburn lunged at Barksdale, aiming to clock him square in the jaw. Instead, he came away holding something soft.

Barksdale's hair.

Or rather, his wig.

For a breathless moment, the chamber froze. Washburn, dumbfounded, handed the thing back. Barksdale, red-faced and rattled, yanked it from his hand and plopped it back on.

Backwards.

Someone laughed. Then another. Even the most stone-faced congressmen broke. The brawl dissolved in a wave of snorts and guffaws. A congressional clerk wrote later that Barksdale's reversed wig may have done more for temporary peace than any speech ever delivered.

But laughter wouldn't follow him forever.

Cemetery Ridge

Five years later, the same man stood in a thunder of cannon fire, charging Union lines at Gettysburg. Barksdale was no longer a loud-mouthed congressman. He was a general now. Confederate. Ruthless. His Mississippi Brigade tore through peach orchards and wheat fields like a sickle in overripe grain.

They said he was wild in battle. Hat off. Sparse hair flying. Screaming at the top of his lungs.

It took a bullet to the knee to slow him. Then a cannonball ripped through his left foot. Still, he clutched his sword. Still, he ordered his men forward.

Only a bullet through the chest brought him down.

Lying in the dirt, mud clogging the fabric of his uniform, Barksdale gasped to his aide:

"I am killed. Tell my wife and children... I died fighting at my post."

That night, Union soldiers found him among the bodies. They carried him to the Jacob Hummelbaugh farmhouse, where a musician-turned-medic named Robert Cassiday held a cup of water to his lips until the morphine finally took.

Barksdale died in the early hours of July 3.

They buried him behind the house in a temporary grave.

But something else stayed behind.

The Hound

In 1867, Barksdale's wife, Narcissa, came to Gettysburg to take his remains home. With her she brought the general's old hunting dog.

As the men lifted the coffin into the wagon, the hound let out a long, soul-bleeding howl.

Then it lay down on the spot where his master had been buried—and would not rise.

Narcissa pleaded. Begged. Called the dog by name. He didn't move.

Locals tried to feed him. Bring him inside when frost came.

He refused all of it.

They found him curled in the grass weeks later. Cold. Still facing south. He died watching over a grave that no longer held a body.

The Haunting

The Hummelbaugh house still stands. The National Park Service owns it. The walls are painted fresh, the fences mended, the lawn trimmed like nothing terrible ever happened there. But after dusk, things change.

They say you can hear the dog first—long before anything else. A low, drawn-out howl that rolls through the orchard like smoke. Not a bark. Not a whimper.

A cry.

Some nights it comes from the tree line. Some nights from beneath the rear window. Always the same: a baying sound stretched too long, like the animal forgot how to stop. Those who stay too long near the yard report more than howls.

They hear panting—wet and close. They hear claws on wood. Scratching at the cellar door. Scraping the frame of the back porch. Clicking across the floorboards, even when no animal's inside.

The house feels colder by the parlor.

And sometimes, when the wind dies, there is no sound at all. Just a shape behind the glass—a wide silhouette, shoulders hunched, no hat, unmoving. A shadow of a man looking in. But then, beside him, something smaller begins to move.

Pacing in slow, silent circles. Waiting. Watching.

Some say the dog's howl isn't mourning at all. That it's calling out—searching, night after night, for a master long buried and gone. A loyalty twisted by death into something restless. It will never stop looking.

But others believe the howl means something else entirely. That it isn't a cry of sorrow.

It's a warning.

They say the dog's baying marks the return of something left behind in the blood-soaked fields—a darker presence that clings to the old farmhouse, drawn by grief, fed by war, eager for more bloodshed. And when the howling comes too close...someone is about to be claimed.

Arch Murderess of Hand Street
(Allegheny County)

Allegheny City (Now Pittsburgh's North Side)
The Woman on the Bridge

She appeared near the old Hand Street Bridge sometime after midnight. Dark dress, lowered head. She shuffled past those who saw her, slow and oblivious, her boots making no sound on the bricks.

At first, no one recognized her.

Then someone did.

And that's when the horror began.

The Kind Neighbor

In 1859, Martha Grinder moved to Pittsburgh from Louisville with her husband, George, a coal miner, and their infant child. They settled in a cramped home near the Point, barely scraping by.

But within months, the family had relocated to a finer part of Allegheny City, near the Allegheny River—Gray's Alley, just above the Hand Street Bridge. Suddenly, Martha wore expensive dresses and mingled with society women. When asked how, she said a wealthy uncle had left her money when her child was born.

She introduced herself as kind. Generous. A nurse to the sick. A comfort to the dying.

Especially the dying.

She had a strange habit of offering to dress the bodies afterward. No one else wanted the job. She volunteered with a smile.

Death Comes Quietly

It started next door at the home of James and Mary Carothers.

Mary fell ill. Martha stepped in, offering soup, milk, and gentle hands. Mary died on August 1, 1865. Mary's husband James grew sick soon after.

That was when the questions started.

Mary's body was exhumed. A coroner found powdered arsenic in her organs. They reopened other deaths—Jane R. Buchanan, a young servant in Martha's home, who had died in agony just a year before. Two of George Grinder's brothers. A neighbor named Marguerite Smith.

All dead. All cared for by Martha.

All poisoned.

She fed them arsenic mixed into buttered toast, warm broth, and sweet milk. Then she stole their valuables. Jewelry. Cash. Even the clothes off their backs.

But it wasn't money that drove her. Not entirely.

During her trial, Martha told the jury: "I love to see death in all its forms and phases, and left no opportunity to gratify my tastes for such sights. Could I have had my own way, probably I should have done more."

They hanged her at the Allegheny County jail on January 19, 1866. She was fifty.

But she was not done.

Ghost in the Fourth Ward

The sightings started almost immediately.

At first, only a few people saw her—those who knew her face. But by 1869, more came forward. The *Pittsburgh Daily Post* reported:

"It is, as if at first, it came reluctantly and under protest to the scene of the deeds that made it so terribly unwelcome, but audacious at length, found a kind of grim delight in spreading a shadowy horror where its tangible horrors of other days were so many and so fell."

One night, a group of young men saw her walk up from the riverbank near the Hand Street Bridge. She looked ordinary at first—until they recognized her. Some had seen her face in court. Others had seen her in the newspaper sketches. She didn't make a sound. Her ribbons didn't stir in the breeze.

Her boots didn't strike the ground.

They could see the brick wall behind her through her body.

And then she vanished into the shadows.

Walking Mist

More sightings followed.

A house servant and her cousin watched in terror as the figure passed their employer's doorstep—black dress, sunken eyes, slow gait. Both said it was Martha Grinder.

One young man followed her.

She turned a corner into Gray's Alley. He caught up, reached out—his hand passed through cold mist.

She kept walking.

Where She Walks Now

Her ghost was seen for years, then faded as quickly as the story of her murders. But the place remains.

You can walk the same path now—along the Three Rivers Heritage Trail near what was once the Hand Street Bridge, now the Ninth Street Bridge or Rachel Carson Bridge.

Sometimes, if you're quiet and the wind is off the water, you may catch the scent of bitter herbs and scorched broth. Or see a figure in black pass between the old iron piers.

If she asks you in for soup—or offers warm milk in a cracked porcelain cup—

Please don't drink it.

She still likes to watch people die.

Dead Man's Hollow
(Allegheny County)

Youghiogheny River Valley, Near McKeesport, Dead Man's Hollow Conservation Area

The trail is quiet now—trees well-kept, gravel tamped down, markers posted by the Allegheny Land Trust. It runs just under a mile from Boston Ballfield Park along the Great Allegheny Passage.

People walk their dogs.

Joggers pass by.

Birdsong cuts through the hush of wind on leaves.

But step off the trail. Just a little. Just far enough to leave the clean gravel behind. The woods grow thicker fast—the land dips. Roots claw the path. You'll find crumbling sandstone walls, rust-colored bricks peeking through the soil, pipes jutting like bones from the creekbank.

This is the part they didn't clean up.

This is Dead Man's Hollow.

Industry and Ruin

From the 1880s through the 1920s, the hollow was a hive of grinding machines and smoke-belching kilns. First came George Flemming's stone quarry. Then, brickworks, pipeworks, crushing plants, and clay kilns.

Men died here every decade.

In 1925, one of the kilns exploded. The factory shut down. The forest swallowed the place whole.

All that remains now are ruins. And the dead.

The Hollow Earns Its Name

The name came before the factories.

In the 1870s, boys exploring the creek valley found a man hanging from a tree. So rotted he had no name. They started calling it *the hollow where the dead man showed up.* That stuck. But he wasn't the last.

The bend in the river makes this a perfect catch basin—where bodies float in from upstream and get trapped in the eddies of Dead Man's Run.

Others ended up here not by accident.

Some were shot. Some were drowned. Some were crushed, burned, or buried alive. They didn't all leave.

A Few of the Lost

January 15, 1874 – John Colson, a mechanic from National Tube Works, was dragged under when a stranger in a capsized skiff gripped him in panic. Neither man surfaced again.

August 2, 1881 – Hardware merchant George McClure was gunned down in the hollow by thieves he tried to track down. His body was found after dark, full of bullets.

March 14, 1883 – George and Daniel Henninger were warming frozen dynamite near a fire when it went off. A reporter wrote: *"Arms and legs hurled hither and thither."*

September 25, 1905 – Mike Sacco, riding the freight elevator of the Union Sewer Pipe Company, got pinned between floors when he tried to jump off as the elevator went the wrong direction. The machinery crushed him.

December 1, 1916 – Hunters chasing the sound of a dog found Samuel Candy face-down in the creek. He'd been shot seven times. Police thought it was revenge. Or maybe love. He had enemies in both directions.

May 26, 1944 – A storm flipped a rowboat. Two women drowned before they could be pulled from the river. One was twenty years old—the other thirty-three.

And then there were peculiar incidents.

August 1893 – Charles Brown saw a giant snake cross the path. He fainted. When he came to, it was gone.

1934 – On a moonlit night, Michael Bendzuch Jr. rowed across the Yough and watched a mist curl onto the far bank. From it stepped a tall figure—a Native American. They stared at each other. Neither moved. Bendzuch never crossed the river at night again.

Things That Linger

People still hear voices in the woods. Low talking with no speaker. Crying, like a baby left somewhere deep in the trees. Shadow figures walk the trail and vanish between trees.

The hollow was a hiding place for bootleggers, robbers, and men with guns and grudges. That energy doesn't go easy. And some of it fights back.

Like Ward McConkey.

McConkey was just nineteen when he was hanged for killing George McClure in the hollow. He swore innocence all the way to the rope. "You hang me because I won't squeal. I'm innocent," he spat his last words. "Goodbye, murderers. Goodbye." They put a white cap over his face. Sprung the trap. But he never really dropped. His voice has been heard on the trail at night—soft, right behind your ear.

Sometimes that's all. Sometimes it's not.

Last Warning

If you find yourself on the wrong path…if the brush grows thick and the red bricks start to show…if the trees close in too tight…if the crying starts or the woods go silent or the fog begins to roll uphill—don't look back.

Don't answer the voice that whispers your name.

And if something breathes beside you and says:

"Goodbye, murderers. Goodbye."

Run. Before you join the others who never made it out of the hollow.

The Centaur of Chickasaw Mine
(Armstrong County)

Widnoon, Old Chickasaw

Chickasaw sat along a tidal spur of the Pittsburgh & Shawmut Railroad, just outside Widnoon. It was a proper boomtown—built around the coal seam, shaped by the rail, and driven by the whistle. Miners worked long hours in the dark, hauling bituminous coal from the rock face to be cleaned, crushed, and shipped to Mahoning. The days were hard but ordinary. Until the ghost came.

The Warning

It happened on Friday, March 7, 1913.

Down in the mine, men began shouting. Lamps shook. Picks fell silent.

Something had come into the tunnels.

They described it later to *The Philadelphia Inquirer*: a wraithlike thing, with the upper body of an emaciated man and the hindquarters of a horse. Pale skin, drawn face. It carried a tin dinner pail, and from it leaked beams of flickering, unnatural light.

It walked between rooms like it knew the place. Calm. Direct. Speaking a single word:

"Go."

Some men dropped their tools and ran. Others stood in terror until the thing passed, its hoofed legs clacking softly on the rock. One by one, they bolted for the exit.

Martel's Escape

John Martel ran the motor.

He saw the thing step into the tunnel ahead, the light from the pail slicing the air.

It pointed at him. "Go."

Martel screamed and fled on foot—but not fast enough. The ghost gave chase, laughing. Not with joy. With something colder. Crueler.

It mounted the motor, threw the throttle, and sent the machine screaming up the rail line—straight to the mouth of the mine.

And there, just before it reached the daylight, it vanished.

The Men Return

The mine didn't close. Too much coal still in the ground. Too many families needing wages.

But no one went back down right away. Days passed before crews returned. Some refused. Others crossed themselves at the shaft entrance.

Men worked more wary after that. Quieter. And deep in the tunnels, even years later, some said they saw flickers of light that didn't belong to any lantern. And heard footsteps that didn't match human feet.

The Thing with the Pail

Some believe it was no ghost at all—something older— a curse on the land or the seam. The centaur shape, they said, was no accident. It meant something.

A beast of burden made from man and mule. Born of toil. Twisted by the weight of too many years in the dark.

It came not to kill. But to warn.

The mine is sealed now. Buried beneath years of earth, rust, and silence. Nothing goes in. Nothing comes out.

But one day, they say, it will come again.

Maybe not in Chickasaw.

Maybe not in Armstrong County.

But somewhere—when the drills go too deep, or the roof starts to crack, or the shadows in the shaft stretch too long—it'll walk the tunnel once more. It will hold out the light. And it will speak only once. "Go."

If you're wise, you'll listen.

If not—you'll hear that laughter chasing you into the dark. And you may never come back.

The Dog That Wasn't There
(Beaver County)

Raccoon Creek, Near Aliquippa – Late 1700s

Rev. George M. Scott was alone.

He'd been riding west, preaching along the Allegheny frontier, when he came to the wooded bends of Raccoon Creek near Aliquippa. The trail narrowed to a trickle of stone and moss. His horse stopped.

There was something up ahead.

A dog.

Or what looked like one.

It wasn't large, but its coat shimmered, as if touched by frost or moonlight—though the sky that evening was thick with cloud. The creature didn't bark. It didn't growl. It simply stood on the path and watched.

Then a noise from the brush—a low snarl, the thump of heavy paws.

A bear.

The hound turned and walked straight toward it. No sound, no fear. The bear crashed back into the woods, retreating fast into the black trees. The dog circled once, looked back at the preacher...and vanished.

No pawprints. No rustle. Just the creek.

Scott crossed quickly and never saw it again.

What It Was

He told the story often, but never claimed it was a ghost. Others filled in the gaps.

Some said it was a guardian spirit—sent to protect a man of faith. Others said it was an omen, a creature of the wild-ways that walks only when the veil is thin.

But those who walk Raccoon Creek now say something still watches from the trail forks.

And if a dog appears in your path—silent, pale, and lit from nowhere—follow it.

It might be the only thing that gets you out.

The White Lady of the Cut
(Beaver County)

Shenango Road, near Chippewa Township
The Bridge

It doesn't look like much now. Just a cracked span of old concrete across a deep rail trench carved back in the 1850s. They call it Summit Cut.

Stone walls line the gorge below. Fog pools there on wet nights—thick, cold, rising from the ground like smoke.

Locals say the place is haunted. They're not wrong.

The First Fall

The first death came in 1894.

Her name was Josephine Cox, and she was riding a buggy near the edge of the cut when a train passed below. The noise spooked the horse. It bolted. The buggy veered off the embankment and rolled down the rocks.

Josephine's body was found broken at the bottom, tangled in the twisted harness.

More to Follow

On November 27, 1951, a 44-year-old woman from Beaver Falls climbed the bridge rail during a storm and jumped.

Less than a year later, in May 1952, a couple lost control in the rain. Their car smashed through the guardrail and dropped to the tracks below.

Neither survived. They say tragedies come in threes. But something about this place wouldn't stop counting.

The Woman in White

When the stories began, nobody can quite recall.

But people crossing Shenango Road at night spoke of lights beneath the bridge, flickering and unnatural. Then came the fog—dense and prickling with some sort of energy, glowing faintly with no moon above. And sometimes, just before midnight, a figure appeared.

A woman. Dressed in white. Soaked to the skin. Walking the rails where the dead fell. Some say it's the woman from the crash. Some say it's the jumper. But those who know the land—who remember the old stories—say it's Josephine.

Still walking.

Still falling.

Again and again.

The Warning

If you stop your car on that bridge during a storm, don't linger.

If you see mist rising from the cut and feel the hair on your arms and nape of neck shoot up, don't get out.

And if you look down and see her—drifting through the fog, her dress dragging behind her on the gravel—

Don't call out.

Don't follow.

And whatever you do... don't lean over the rail.

Because once she looks up—you're hers.

And you will join them below.

The Green Man of Route 351
(Beaver County)

Route 351—Koppel

On the outskirts of Pittsburgh, where the Pennsylvania Railroad's Peters Creek Branch once clattered through the coal-stained hills, a tunnel became the center of one of Pennsylvania's most chilling legends.

Locals whispered that if you stopped your car in the black mouth of the tunnel, switched off the headlights, and called his name, something would answer.

They said a figure would emerge—a man glowing faintly green, his outline unsteady in the dark. Sometimes he brushed the hood of the car. Engines would die, lights would sputter, and terrified drivers found themselves trapped in a tomb of silence with something unnatural moving closer.

The Folklore

The story told of an electrician from Dravosburg, electrocuted in a violent accident atop the tunnel. His body, they said, was scorched by the current until his skin itself glowed with a ghastly green light.

His ghost wandered the tunnel afterward, forever marked by the way he died.

But legends often hide something deeper, and in this case, the horror was not born in the tunnel at all. It began years earlier, with a boy named Raymond Robinson.

The True Horror

On June 18, 1919, eight-year-old Raymond climbed the Morado Bridge with a child's fearlessness, reaching for a bird's nest perched dangerously near the lines of the Beaver Valley Traction Company. In one blinding flash, 11,000 volts tore through his body.

The surge burned him beyond recognition—his eyes gone, his nose melted away, his lips and cheeks reduced to an unshaped hole. One arm was destroyed nearly to the elbow. Doctors did not expect him to live.

But Raymond survived.

He grew into a man who rarely showed himself by day. Instead, he walked the back roads of Beaver County at night—along Route 351, the Koppel–New Galilee Road.

Alone, he tapped the pavement with a walking stick, one bare foot feeling the road's edge so he would not lose his way. His face startled those who met him: eyeless sockets, scarred flesh, and silence broken only when he forced speech through the ruined opening of his mouth.

The Legend Grows

By the 1950s and 1960s, word spread of a phantom figure wandering Route 351 in the dark. Headlights would catch him for only a moment: a faceless man, glowing faintly, vanishing into the night. Some fled in terror. Others dared to stop and speak to him. They called him the Green Man, or more cruelly, Charlie No-Face.

Those who met him remembered not horror, but kindness. He would sometimes smile, as best he could, and even pose for pictures. Yet the image burned into memory—the eyeless, glowing figure haunting Pennsylvania's back roads—outlived the man himself.

After Death

Raymond Robinson died quietly in 1984, at age 74. But the legend did not die. The tunnel on Peters Creek and the still draws curious seekers who honk their horns, switch off their lights, and wait. Others drive Route 351, scanning the darkness and searching for the Green Man. Some claim they still see him: a faceless man glowing faintly in the dark, wandering as he always did, caught forever between folklore and nightmare.

And when the silence grows heavy inside the tunnel, locals say you can feel him moving closer, as though his scarred hand might brush across your car in the dark.

The Green Man walks still.

The Ghost Dog of Eschelman Cemetery
(Bedford County)

Leather Cracker, Eschelman Cemetery—Hickory Bottom Road on Morrison's Cove

Nestled in Leather Cracker (now Henrietta), Eschelman Cemetery is old—its first stones dating to the early 1800s. It sits quietly on Hickory Bottom Road, hidden in the folds of Morrison's Cove. In those days, death sat close to the soil. But no one expected a dog's phantom to rise from those graves.

The First Sightings

Between 1815 and 1820, locals began whispering about a large black dog that emerged from the cemetery at dawn. It followed passersby—its eyes mournful, tail tucked low, pacing beside their wagon wheels or walking boots.

Then, as suddenly as it appeared, it vanished—always just beyond the churchyard fence.

Witnesses insisted: this was no stray. Its ribs showed through its coat. Its gait begged for reunion.

And—oddest of all—it disappeared at the boundary of the graveyard, as though the living world couldn't hold it.

A Child's Ghostly Encounter

In March 1923, *The Altoona Tribune* printed Lydia Miller's account: a little girl of 12, once bringing cows to pasture, heard footsteps behind her. She turned—and saw that same shadowed beast. A black dog, tall, narrow-chested. Its head was low, its ears pinned back, and its eyes fixed on her. She ran.

But the dog did not chase. It simply walked behind her, mile after mile, morning after morning. Eventually, Lydia stopped running.

What It Wanted

One morning near the edge of the pasture, the dog came closer than usual. It stepped forward slowly—then rose onto its hind legs, as if to greet her like a friendly pet. Lydia said she felt no fear in that moment—only sadness. Still, she flinched—instinctively throwing up her arms to shield herself. And just like that, it vanished.

The Graveyard That Keeps Its Own

Rumor says the dog belonged to a murderer buried there—tying its spirit to a restless soul chained to sin.

In Pennsylvania Dutch tradition, killers stayed close to where they shed blood. So perhaps their loyal dog stayed too, watching, silent, waiting for a master who never returned.

Others say it was a gentle shepherd—protecting graves from vandals, from the living who forgot to remember.

The Omen on Hickory Bottom Road

Even now, those who pass the cemetery at dawn or dusk speak of something wrong in the air. Not fear exactly—something heavier. Like sorrow turned sour.

They hear the soft drag of paws over frost-bitten earth. See a shape just ahead in the fog, holding still in the silence. Its eyes catch the light—not red, not white—just a dull, waiting glint.

Some say the dog walks only with children.

But others... it watches. And though few stop to look, many feel it: that shift in the dusk, that sense of being marked. We don't know what it's waiting for. Or who. Some whisper it follows those with guilt on their shoulders. Others say it sniffs out the ones who have something to hide. But no one can say what happens if it steps off the path.

Because those it chooses never speak of it.

And some never come back.

The Debt that Would Not Die
(Bedford County)

An Old Long-gone House in Bedford

In the 1800s, around Bedford, two men were known to pass the time over cards: Abraham Coon and Conrad Haverstock. Friends, most days. Drinkers, always. One Sunday, they played for a dollar's worth of liquor. Coon lost. No coin in his pocket, he borrowed from Haverstock, who left to fetch the bottle. Coon, ashamed, meant to repay it before sundown. But before he could, his wife screamed from the doorway—his child was dying.

In haste, he buried the silver at the root of a tree. He never dug it back up. He fell sick that same day and died before the week was out.

The Visit

A year passed. Then another. In 1819, a pious woman named Miss Sills, living near Bedford, began to see a man in her room. He said nothing at first. Just stared, dark and swarthy, heavy with smoke. She knew him from town—Abraham Coon.

But Abraham Coon was dead.

The spirit returned three times before she dared speak. When she did, he gave her a task.

Retrieve the buried coin. Deliver it to Haverstock—now moved to Tuscarawas County, Ohio.

If she refused, she would be cursed to wander, unable to enter her home or live within a hundred miles of it for three years.

She obeyed. She and her uncle found the coin beneath the roots and traveled 200 miles west. But when she placed the coin in Haverstock's hand, he laughed bitterly.

"It was never owed," he said.

He tossed the coin to the ground.

The Coin That Would Not Stay Buried

Some days later, Esquire Knicely found the tarnished silver in the dirt and slipped it into his coat. He thought little of it—until, while burning brush in the woods, he was approached by a rider. The horse was black. The man upon it was darker still—his voice hollow, as though funneled through an iron pipe.

"Have you the coin owed to Haverstock?"

Knicely reached into his pocket, trembling. The coin lay in his palm.

"Return it," the ghost intoned.

Then, in a flash of fire, he vanished.

Knicely tried. But Haverstock again refused.

So, the ghost returned. Again. And again. Each time more forceful. Each time colder.

Finally, Knicely's father intervened, begged the man to take the coin—to end it. Haverstock relented. The coin was placed on the windowsill of his house.

And that, they say, was enough.

But It Was Never Forgotten by the Dead

Years passed. The house crumbled. The coin remained. Tarnished. Forgotten by the living. Not so, by the dead.

Someone picked it up.

And now it's waiting again. For a name. For a debt. For a hand to carry it forward.

Beware the coin you find where no coin should be.

Beware, the silver turned black.

Because this time, the ghost won't rest.

There is no one left to pay the debt.

Only you.

And ghosts don't forgive. Nor do they ever forget.

Lost Children of the Alleghenies
(Bedford County)

On the Edge of Blue Knob State Park

The land was untouched then. Before the saw came, before the earth was stripped bare, the woods in Bedford County stood ancient and thick—black-trunked and swaying like giants that whispered to themselves. In that deep silence of April 24, 1856, the first sounds of horror began as nothing more than a dog's bark.

Samuel Cox rose from his bed at dawn, musket in hand, thinking his hounds had treed a squirrel in the brush. He followed their call into the woods behind his home in Spruce Hollow, his boots sinking into thawed earth still slick from the snowmelt. He was gone long enough to lose the hush of morning—but when he came back, something was already wrong.

His wife, Susannah, pale and shaking, met him at the door. "Where are the boys?" Joseph, five. George, seven.

She thought they had followed him, as children often did. But the forest had not held their laughter that morning. It had swallowed them.

And it did not give them back. At least not to the living.

The Search Becomes a Mob

By sundown, over a thousand people roamed the woods, torches in hand. They carved search lines across the hills and ravines, waded through swollen Bobb's Creek, shouting their names into the void. Nothing answered. No footprints. No broken branches. Just cold forest and that rising, awful dread that perhaps the land itself had taken the boys.

Two days passed, and suspicion bloomed like rot. Neighbors accused the parents—whispers turned into jeers. *They're lying. Trying to gain sympathy, money... something's not right.* Men turned on the grieving. The Cox cabin was searched top to bottom, floorboards pried up, the well examined. No blood. No tiny bones. No trace of what had become of the boys.

Out of desperation, a dowser was called in.

Then a witch.

They said strange things. Drew symbols in the dirt. None helped. None found them.

The Dream

Then came May 2. A nearby farmer, Jacob Dibert, pale and troubled, claimed he had seen something in his sleep. A vision—too vivid to be mere dream. He alleged that he saw himself walking through a thick ravine. A fallen deer lay rotting in the leaves. Then a small shoe. A swollen stream, crossed by a downed tree. Beyond it: a white birch, its limbs curled like fingers. And beneath it—the boys. Cold. Still. Facedown in the earth.

Dibert told no one at first, except his wife and brother-in-law, Harrison Whysong. The three set out together and followed the dream's path like bloodhounds.

It led them true.

Just as he had seen: the deer carcass. The shoe. The stream and the bridge of wood. The white birch. And beneath it—the bodies.

Joseph and George. Faces bloated, skin waxen, lips blue. Their hands frozen mid-reach. One stilled by a sob, mouth filled with dirt. They said there were no marks of violence; no sign of struggle. They lay miles from home, cold and alone.

Dibert told the others he had dreamed it. Nobody questioned. Nobody suspected. Nobody doubted.

What the Earth Keeps

Some say they died of exposure. Lost and starved in the wet cold. But they had crossed a roaring creek. Miles of woods. They said that they were found lying side by side, as if they had been placed that way.

Did anybody doubt the man's alleged dream was real? Because nowadays, many do. Did he see their bodies...or leave them there? Guilt? Glee? Or was he good and true?

Who dreams the *exact* path to a grave?

The mystery has never been solved.

And the forest has never told.

And Still They Whisper

Locals say the Cox boys are not done.

Sometimes near Bobb's Creek, when the snow is melting and the woods still bare, you'll hear something—giggling, soft-footed running through brush.

Then the shrieking.

Then nothing.

Something always waits beneath that birch.

Not all creatures leave tracks.

Some wear the skin of men.

Some walk in dreams.

And some take children.

Still.

Ghost of the Irish Creek Bridge
(Berks County)

Leesport–Mohrsville

The Errand That Never Finished

On the morning of October 8, 1857, a passerby found the body of 19-year-old Adeline Baver under the Pennsylvania & Reading Railroad bridge in a bloodied, muddy puddle spanning Irish Creek. A domestic servant for several families in the area, she'd vanished the night before.

Her chest was cut in deep, harsh gashes.

Her throat was violently slit. She was last seen alive by railroad workers, to whom she mentioned that she was on an errand as she passed by.

Adeline was traveling to Reading to meet a man named Mr. Shelly at the agricultural fair, where she intended to pick up a gold watch she had left at his family's home.

Unfortunately, she never made it to Reading.

The Search by the Creek

Authorities scoured the area and followed signs of a struggle: a hidden island on the Schuylkill River, where blood pooled beneath a felled tree. Her gold earrings were found in the brush.

She had been moved.

Tracks in the mud led back toward the bridge, suggesting she'd been dragged there after death—staged to mislead. A final patch of churned earth and stained grass marked where she must have fallen—or collapsed.

A white linen shirt and a coarse cotton undershirt splashed with blood were uncovered in a hole near the scene of the brutal slaying, waiting to rot away to nothing.

A short distance away, they found another stain where she'd bled out.

They realized the truth.

She had been killed in the woods and carried through the brush.

Her body posed beneath the bridge—left to be mistaken for a train accident.

Justice Served?

Three men were arrested and jailed: David Gumbert, Samuel Hyler, and Jackson Williams (alias Tom Williams). All were charged in the brutal crime. Another man, Baetzel, a brakeman for the railroad, was initially arrested and then released. He was said to have died in a rail accident… until someone saw him alive, thirty years later, in another town. In 1875, a man named John Ezra Lovering, sentenced to hang for another killing, confessed to Adeline's murder on the gallows in Mifflintown. He gave details of her death, naming her directly. However, the confession was never followed up on. By then, the case had long gone cold.

The Ghost of Irish Creek Bridge

Adeline was buried in the old cemetery. But her ghost stays on. Beneath the Irish Creek bridge, in the last light of day, the mist sometimes gathers low—thick, unnatural, as if exhaled from the ground itself. In that gray veil, a figure appears. White. Still.

Slumped forward at the shoulders, her dress soaked to the hem in black creek mud. She stands just beyond the rails, unmoving. And then, slowly, her head turns.

No one knows why she returns. Was justice truly served? Or does she walk because something remains unfinished—something buried deeper than the body?

Some believe she waits for another to fall. Others think she's there to warn. But all agree on one thing: if you see her face too clearly…you might not forget it.

Even when you close your eyes.

Butcher of Hawk Mountain
(Berks County)

Schaumboch's Tavern on Hawk Mountain

High on a ridge in the Blue Mountains stands a crumbling tavern with rot in its bones. Its keeper, Matthias Schaumboch, was no innkeeper—he was a butcher of men. Travelers who stopped for ale and sleep were drugged, stripped of goods, and hacked apart in their beds. Fourteen, he confessed on his deathbed. Some say more. When they buried him, lightning struck. The coffin flipped face-down.

Since then, locals say Schaumboch's spirit roams. Lights flicker through shuttered windows. Boots pace an empty cellar. And sometimes, from the staircase— A girl in white descends, never touching the floor, never reaching the bottom.

She was never listed among the dead.

The Grotesque Spectacle of Horseshoe Curve
(Blair County)

Horseshoe Curve & Bennington Wreck | Altoona

The Horseshoe Curve, carved into the Allegheny spine in 1854, was a triumph of rail engineering—a coiled ascent that let heavy trains claw their way westward. But it came at a cost. Built with picks, shovels, and dynamite, its dirt was soaked with the sweat of immigrants and the blood of the broken. They called it progress.

The mountain called it something else.

It's never been kind to the living.

The Ones Who Went Under

In December 1909, Edward Allison, a 22-year-old brakeman, slipped from his train and went down between the rails. His wife was told he died quick. But men who gathered the pieces said his body kept moving for several feet—dragged and sheared, folded beneath wheels until there was nothing left to cradle.

In 1916, fog swallowed the tracks like a lungful of smoke. A brakeman and a conductor stood waiting for their next car. An empty freight train punched through the mist without a sound. By the time it passed, the men were pulp in the gravel.

Then came October 1934. A seasoned fireman stepped down to pick up a dropped flare. His boot hit oil. The wet iron took him down. The weight of his own locomotive rolled over his hips and shoulders. He screamed for ten seconds straight. That's what they said.

They buried what they could find in a canvas sack.

The Red Arrow Disaster

A few miles west of the Curve, just below Sugar Run at Bennington Curve, the mountain claimed more.

February 18, 1947. Just after 3:20 a.m.

Train No. 68, the Red Arrow, hit the bend too fast. The steel couldn't hold. Both locomotives and eleven of fourteen passenger cars flew from the rails—some jackknifing, some tumbling end over end down a 100-foot embankment.

They found passengers laying mangled in twisted coach frames. Mail clerks were crushed against sorting racks. Some never had a chance to scream.

Twenty-four dead—15 passengers, 6 mail clerks, and 3 crew members One hundred thirty-one injured.

Most never saw it coming.

The Haunting That Followed

In the years since, something lingers on that curve.

Workers hear voices just before dawn—soft and close, like someone seated beside them. Names whispered in the wind. Sometimes it's "help me." Sometimes it's just breathing.

Others see figures standing where the cars left the rails. Unmoving. Gray. Watching the tracks like they're waiting to be called.

Approach them, and they vanish into the rock.

On cold anniversaries, that section of rail sometimes reeks of scorched wool and burning oil. There's frost on the trees. Snow on the embankment. But the smell hangs like smoke in a sealed room.

It hasn't gone away.

And the mountain still takes what it wants. It chews them up—flesh, steel, and soul—and spits them out as ghosts, like some obscene pie-eating contest. But this crowd isn't clapping. There's no laughter, no mess of crust and cherry filling. Just bodies—broken and burned—and the crowd is us. Standing still. Watching in silence, mouths agape, horror in our eyes... waiting to see who gets served next.

White Lady of the Horseshoe Curve Tunnel
(Blair County)

Horseshoe Curve Tunnel outside Altoona

Five miles west of Altoona, the world twists unnaturally. There, the Horseshoe Curve railway bends around a manmade lake, a towering dam, and the highest of three Altoona reservoirs. Trains grind and howl along the arc—a feat of iron and will, cut straight into the spine of the Alleghenies. And beneath it all, something waits.

The Tunnel Below

Long before cars ever passed through it, the tunnel beneath Horseshoe Curve was cut for wagons and horses—a narrow stone underpass built in the 1850s alongside the curve's construction. It was never meant for speed. Just a quiet way through the valley for those too slow or too fragile to cross the rails above.

But time kept moving.

The wagons gave way to Fords, and the underpass grew slick with oil and exhaust. Still, the bones of the old way remained—arched stone, dripping walls, the sense that something older clung to the mortar.

The Deaths Came Early. And Often.

Many more were lost during the Curve's construction in 1850, when men, most unnamed, dug with picks, shovels, and blistered hands. No heavy machines. Just stone, sweat—and the ones the mountain kept.

One of them had a wife.

The Woman Who Waited Too Long

Each evening, she came down from the hills to meet him. Walked the ridge with her coat pulled close, a basket swinging at her side. But he never returned.

After the rockslide took him, she came anyway. And after she died, she still came.

Workers reported a pale figure gliding through the tunnel mouth, just beyond the lantern light. Head bowed. Skirt brushing the stones. Sometimes she turned. Sometimes she waited. The White Lady, they called her.

She didn't cry.

She didn't speak. But those who looked too long said their ears filled with the sound of gravel shifting... and the low wet cough of someone drowning in blood.

But those who pass say something follows. A feeling like being watched.

They say it's her. Still waiting. And if she turns and looks at you—don't wave. Don't speak. Don't stop.

The Ritual and the Warning

Decades later, thrill seekers drove up at midnight with horns and flashlights—

One wrote:

"I felt... heavy. Not scared at first, just sick. Then the battery died. Then we heard it—metal clanging, like hammering, like carts. Then voices. Then... figures through the trees."

They left fast. Later, they found long handprints smeared across their car windows. As if something tried to hold on.

Others claimed their radios jumped to static—always after the tunnel. Always after midnight.

Some say she's just mourning.

Others say she's searching for the one who left her behind.

And others still believe that she doesn't walk alone anymore. And she might be looking for you to join her.

Legend of the White Lady of Wopsononock Mountain
(Blair County)

Altoona—Wopsononock Mountain (Devil's Elbow)

The tale of the White Lady has haunted Wopsononock Mountain for more than a century.

Its roots stretch back into the early 20th century, whispered along the winding, forest-choked roads that snake up the Allegheny spine.

The most common telling is simple but devastating:

A young bride, newly wed and filled with promise, was traveling the mountain roads with her husband.

Accounts differ—some say a crash, others that the groom was killed in a sudden accident or robbery—but all end the same. The woman was left alone. Shattered.

Dressed still in her wedding gown, she wandered the shadowed slopes, searching, calling, refusing to leave the place where love was torn from her.

Some claim she perished there—by exposure, grief, or her own hand.

She never left.

Some say the ground itself is stained with her anguish—her footsteps leaving patches of frost, her cries echoing like a warning through the trees. On moonless nights, those who dare to stop along the mountain's edge claim to see blood streaks in the mist, or catch a glimpse of her face twisted in a mask of suffering. There are whispers that those who meet her gaze are doomed to relive her agony in fevered nightmares, waking to phantom bruises or the icy grip of hands around their throats.

The Ghostly Presence

For generations, the mountain has been cursed with her sorrow. Her pale figure lingers in the mists, bound to the twisting roads and silent trees.

Witnesses tell of: A translucent woman in a long white gown, stepping from the roadside fog, vanishing the moment headlights strike her.

Bone-deep cold filling cars, so sharp and unnatural it leaves breath steaming inside the windows.

Hitchhiker tales—a woman in white flagging down drivers, but disappearing before she can be picked up.

Marks of the dead—a foggy handprint pressed against glass, a sudden sobbing voice in the backseat, the scent of damp roses lingering though no flowers are near.

One chilling account preserved in a local Blair County Facebook group echoes the older oral tales:

"We were driving up Wopsy late at night when we saw this woman in a long white dress standing by the side of the road. As soon as our headlights hit her, she vanished into the trees. I'll never forget how cold it felt in the car after that."

The Curse of Wopsy

The mountain itself seems steeped in her anguish. Fog clings thicker here, trees bend inward, and silence falls too heavily on the winding road. Old-timers warn that to see her is to invite misfortune—wrecks, illness, or worse.

They say her grief turned venomous.

They say she doesn't just wander.

She waits.

The Rise of the Mining Dead: Barclay Cemetery
(Bradford County)

Barclay on Barclay Mountain— Abandoned by 1902

Barclay Mountain was once nothing more than dense wildland—quiet, untouched, and cold. But that changed in 1812, when a hunter named Absalom Carr struck coal while tracking game. Word spread fast. What followed wasn't progress—it was conquest. The forest gave way to pits, powder houses, and rail lines.

By 1856, the town of Barclay had grown from nothing into a mining colony perched fifteen hundred feet above Towanda, surrounded by snow-choked woods and hills that blocked the sun until late morning.

"In winter the mountain presents a weird appearance, being thickly wooded and snow capped between the hills, no sunshine until a late hour in the morning. It is therefore much colder than many surrounding places, although very healthy." —*Elmira Advertiser, February 8, 1882*

Stores, shops, churches, schools, and mills popped up. Miners and their families came up the mountain— mostly Irish immigrants: the Mannix, O'Keefe, Roche, Dobbins, Dalton, Carroll, and Sheehan families. The homes were built quick and plain. Four schoolhouses taught 300 children. One general store sold $100,000 a year in goods.

"The town is like all mining places, built up of cheap frame buildings, the residences of the miners. However they are all well arranged and make comfortable homes for the occupants." —*Elmira Advertiser, February 8, 1882*

"The population of the village is about fourteen hundred... All are miners or their families except officers of the mining company and the people of the store and the post master and school teachers, of the latter there are four, all of whom belong elsewhere." —*Elmira Advertiser, February 8, 1882*

But the air was always thin, the wind sharp, and the ground never stopped shifting. They say the living made their homes too close to the dead.

Or maybe there were just so many dead that they crept up on the living.

By 1902, Barclay was gone. Abandoned. Swallowed by cold and collapse. All that remains now is the cemetery—and what's still stirring in the ground below.

Cemetery of Sinkholes and Whispers

Barclay Cemetery lies buried in the heart of State Game Lands 12. No signs remain of the old town. Even St. Patrick's Church is gone, once at the cemetery's edge. All that's left are the headstones, many sinking. The land underneath was mined deep. Tunnels collapsed. Vaults shifted. Now the graves themselves are caving in.

People come up here sometimes—hikers, ghost hunters, or those just curious enough. Not all return easy.

Footsteps echo where there are none to make them.

Whistling winds through the tombstones—but it carries a melody.

Figures in white drift between the graves, vanishing if approached.

In 1999, ghost hunters reported a sound deep in the woods: "A sharp ping—like a pickaxe hitting rock. Then another. And another."

They kept walking, but the sound moved with them.

Some claim to hear children laughing under the trees. Others feel watched from the tree line. The ground is soft in places. You might think it's just water damage—until you step too hard and realize there's nothing beneath you. Just hollow.

Doan Outlaws and the Cave That Wouldn't Let Them Go
(Bucks County)

Ralph Stover State Park & Fleecydale Road—1783

During the Revolutionary War, the Doan Gang—five brothers and a cousin—became the most feared outlaws in southeastern Pennsylvania. They were Loyalists who remained faithful to the British Crown, but they were not soldiers. They robbed tax collectors, plundered militias, and stole horses from Patriot farms.

The Doans grew up in Plumstead Township—Quakers who were disowned for refusing pacifism and turning to violence. By 1783, they had stolen from more than thirty homes and taken hundreds of horses, leaving their neighbors crippled in the growing and selling of crops. They famously raided Newtown's treasury and hid in a limestone cave above Tohickon Creek, now within Ralph Stover State Park. Locals called them "Tories." But some whispered "ghosts," even while they lived. Because they vanished into the cliffs—and no one could catch them.

Until they did.

Doan's Cave

The cave still exists. Known locally as Doan's Cave, it lies in a wooded gorge above the creek. Its existence was first linked to the outlaws by 19th-century historian John P. Rogers, who claimed the gang hid there in the summer of 1783. According to Rogers and later historians, they used the cave until they ran out of supplies. Then they moved southeast to Halsey's Cabin, hoping for rest.

They didn't get it.

The Death of Moses Doan

On the morning of August 27, 1783, a Loyalist sympathizer gave up the gang's location. Bucks County sheriff's men surrounded Halsey's Cabin, a cousin's farmhouse near Hinkletown. Moses Doan, the most feared of the gang, was asleep in the hayloft. He never woke. They shot him in the chest. There was no trial.

Three Doans were captured and hanged the following year. One fled to Canada. One disappeared.

But Moses died violently, in hiding, after fleeing the cliffs and cave that had kept him safe for so long.

The Cave's Mark

In 1859, schoolchildren from Buckingham Township reported seeing an inscription carved in stone inside a local cave: "1775 M"

Locals long believed it marked the presence of Moses Doan. Passed down through generations, the story tied the Doan legend to stone, even as the carving itself faded from view.

In 2024, archaeologists unearthed a matching carved stone near Buckingham. It read the same: "1775 M"

The artifact now rests in a private collection. The connection to Moses remains probable—but still open to interpretation.

Oral Tradition: The Phantom Rider

Locals have long passed down a ghost story: that a man on horseback rides Fleecydale Road at night, his figure seen near the ravine that runs toward the Doans' former hideout. The road curves below the cliffs of Ralph Stover—less than two miles from the cave.

What Remains

The Doans were hunted, killed, and buried in unmarked or distant graves. Their story is carved into Bucks County soil—through court records, newspaper accounts, and stones left behind. But their name lingers in the cliffs. The cave hasn't collapsed. And the road below still turns dark at dusk. The cave is real. The rider is remembered. And Moses never left the ridge.

Old Red Eyes at Conrad Snyder Cemetery
(Butler County)

Conrad Snyder Cemetery
The Swiss Grave on the Hill

The man who first cleared the trees and staked the stones was Conrad Snyder, born in Switzerland around 1735. He brought his family to Pennsylvania sometime before the Revolution, settling on high ground in what would become Brady Township.

Decades passed as the woods gradually reclaimed most of the land—but the cemetery endured.

Conrad was buried there in 1827, nearly fifty years after he arrived. His son was laid to rest just below him, and over the years others joined them. Today, the stones are nearly gone: sunken, lichen-covered, and tucked in a thicket off Burton Road. The site is now barely marked and rarely visited.

But something still walks the hill.

Ol' Red Eyes

Locals call it Ol' Red Eyes. It's unclear how long the name has been passed down. In the 1970s, some kids from Slippery Rock ran screaming from the woods, claiming they saw two red lights hovering near a grave. At first, no one believed them—until others independently reported similar sightings that same decade.

It never comes close. It doesn't chase. It just watches. Always near the largest stone.

That's where Conrad Jr. is buried.

What the Old Folks Said

Some in the area believe it's not a ghost at all, but something older.

A guardian.

A holdover from the old country.

In the mountains of Switzerland—where Conrad was born—they speak of Augenbrand: the Fire-Eyed One. A black dog with eyes like coal, who guards burial sites that are left untended or defiled.

In the Jura hills, they say it walks the bridges where blood was spilled unjustly, protecting the bones beneath.

When Conrad came to this country, he may have brought more than a headstone tradition with him.

Witness accounts say activity started after an act of vandalism in the mid-20th century—stones knocked over, names scraped off, a grave split clean in two. After that, the air grew heavier. Longtime local visitors suddenly turned back at the gate. The eyes began to appear more often, always in the same place, always watching.

Some believe whatever it is wasn't meant to haunt the living—only to guard the dead.

The Cemetery Today

Snyder Cemetery sits inside Moraine State Park now, cut off from the old Snyder land. Visitors say they feel watched, even in daylight. Some say they've seen a green light flicker just over the grass.

But the stories always return to the same thing: "Two red eyes. Low to the ground. Still. Never blinking."

It doesn't haunt the place.

It guards it.

And it remembers who doesn't show respect.

The Rolling Mill Mine: What Waits
(Cambria County)

Rolling Mill Mine in Johnstown– July 10, 1902

Coal mines are closed worlds—cut off from wind and rain, sealed by rock.

But gas moves through them like breath.

Methane gathers in pockets—between coal seams, behind stone ribs—silent, invisible, waiting. When fire meets gas down there, it doesn't explode once.

It detonates, echoes, folds back on itself—igniting coal dust, swallowing oxygen, and leaving afterdamp—a choking blend of carbon monoxide and silence.

That's what happened beneath the Westmont hillside, in the Klondike section of the Rolling Mill Mine, on July 10, 1902. The mine had opened in 1856, carved to feed coal into the Cambria Iron Company's steelworks across the river. That day, it fed on men instead.

The Last Shift

The explosion killed 112 miners, mostly immigrants—Slovak, Hungarian, Polish. Some died in the first blast. Others were burned. Most suffocated, deeper in. It took hours before rescuers could reach them—their lamps dimming in pockets of poison. What they found were bodies curled in side tunnels, hands still grasping lunch tins, faces frozen as if in prayer.

The 112 miners who perished in the explosion and the ensuing afterdamp were recovered and removed from the mine.

The tunnel was sealed. The hillside was left to settle. But something lingered.

The Trail Now

The old coal route has become the James Wolfe Sculpture Trail—a winding climb that snakes between the top and bottom of the Johnstown Inclined Plane. Sculptures stand watch among the trees. The air gets colder as you go up.

Near the mine's old entrance—now sealed by concrete and rust—some say the air changes. It drops. It thickens. And sometimes, it moves.

The Boy in 1992

In 1992, a 10-year-old boy walking the trail with his mother stopped and pointed. He asked who the men were. The ones with blackened faces and tin pails.

He didn't know about the mine. Didn't know 112 men had died under that same ridge. Didn't know the entrance was right behind them.

The Ones Still Working

Visitors still talk—quietly.

They say they've seen figures on the trail.

Thin. Slow.

Stooped like men at shift's end.

Some carry buckets.

Some wear caps.

None speak.

They don't look at everyone.

But if they do single someone out—it means they've seen something in them. Not the past. *The future.*

They don't move. They don't beckon. They just tarry, silent at the mouth of the mine, for the one carrying something dark ahead.

A warning, maybe, for something dark on their horizon.

But who it's for...that's the part no one ever knows.

Until they approach.

The Puppeteer
(Cameron County)

Old Lumber Camps

In the shadowed lumber camps of Cameron and Clinton Counties, they remembered the wagon before they remembered the man.

Canvas-topped, streaked in pitch and soot, it came late—after the felling season, when the timber crews were half-starved and bone-sore, and the sky had already gone gray.

Peter Hauntz, he called himself.

But veterans' rolls and court ledgers knew him better as James H. Sharp—Company C, 52nd Regiment, Pennsylvania Infantry. He was a Union man with a thousand-yard stare and hands too steady for someone who'd seen what he had.

No one ever saw him carve.

But the puppets came.

The Puppets That Weren't

No one agreed on what they were made of.

Hauntz said black walnut, stained with oxblood. But there were always whispers that human blood was mixed in as well. Because they moved too well. A surgeon's assistant once claimed he saw a wrist flex, too smooth to be string or rod. Another man—drunk, but sober-eyed—swore one blinked during a performance in Driftwood.

The camps had a saying after that: *If it watches you, don't stay after the curtain.*

The star of the show was Herodia. Ballerina. Fortune-teller. Hauntz said she appeared one night in 1873, curled in the back of his wagon, hiding from "people who meant her harm." She danced in near silence. Eyes wide. Mouth never moved. For four years she performed like that—then she was gone.

Asked what happened, Hauntz only muttered: "Some spirits aren't meant to linger."

Hublersburg and the Final Curtain

Later, he returned to Hublersburg, to a drafty house with drawn drapes and trunks no one ever saw opened.

A single candle burned in the upstairs window—always. Even when the house was cold. Even when weeks passed without sign of him.

He died in 1912.

But some said the curtain in that window still moved.

In 1941, a minister named Reverend Dietrich told the *Altoona Tribune* the house gave him chills "no winter could cause." He remembered a tall, dark-eyed girl who traveled with Hauntz.

"She didn't age," he said. "She just vanished."

The Molly Maguires And the Peculiar Handprint

(Carbon County)

Jim Thorpe/Mauch Chunk –1870s

They said the Molly Maguires were a secret society of Irish coal miners, but for the men choking on coal dust in the dark shafts of Schuylkill, Carbon, Luzerne, and Lackawanna counties, there was nothing secret about their rage. Peaceful petitions had done nothing.

Strikes were crushed with bullets.

The coal companies controlled every breath a miner took—from the blackened air underground to the overpriced company store, the only place they could use the scrip they were paid. Their families starved in rotting shanties while the operators built mansions on the backs of broken men.

No one could prove the Mollies existed in the way the owners claimed. Historians now argue it was less an organization than a label—used to silence anyone who fought back. By the 1870s, the mines had grown restless.

Supervisors were found beaten.

Company property burned.

Men began to vanish in the woods.

Someone had to hang for it.

The Trials in Mauch Chunk

Between 1876 and 1878, twenty men were tried and executed for crimes tied to the Molly Maguires. The most infamous trials took place in Mauch Chunk—now called Jim Thorpe—inside the thick stone walls of the Carbon County Jail.

The evidence came almost entirely from a single Pinkerton agent, James McParland. He infiltrated the miners for nearly two years. The trials were bought and paid for by the coal companies. The defendants barely spoke English. Most had no proper defense. Juries were stacked. Sentences rushed.

It was justice built on fear and money.

Seven of those men were hanged right there inside the jail.

On June 21, 1877—"The Day of the Rope"—four of them were led to the gallows. Alexander Campbell. Michael Doyle. Edward Kelly. John Donohue. The gallows floor dropped. The jailers waited for the twitching to stop. No priest was called to bless the dead.

The bodies were taken out the back in wheelbarrows.

The Handprint on the Wall

Alexander Campbell insisted to the end that he was innocent. In the hours before his death, locked in a narrow cell on the second floor, he slapped his mud-caked hand against the plaster and said it would remain as proof—"This mark will stay until Judgment Day."

They painted over it. It came back.

They scrubbed it with acid. It returned.

They tore the plaster down to the brick.

The mark reappeared.

It's still there. A full hand, flat against the wall, fingers outstretched. Not faded. Not smudged. As if someone left it just hours ago.

People who visit that cell say it's never warm, no matter the season. The wall near the handprint always sweats.

Haunted Stone

The Carbon County Jail stands today as a museum. The iron bars are rusted. The air inside is still and stale. But some say the dead never left.

Visitors hear heavy footsteps above them on the gallows floor—when no one is upstairs. Others feel the sudden crush of cold air. Doors slam without warning.

Voices drift from empty cells, murmuring in accents long dead. Tour guides report lights flickering, chairs scraping across the floor, and something pacing in the cell where Campbell once stood.

Some nights, after closing, the security system picks up motion in the old hallway.

There's nothing on the cameras—just darkness, and the faint sound of rope creaking.

Something Still Walks in the Barrens
(Centre County)

Scotia Barrens—State Game Lands 176

The sun was cruelly bright on April 25, 1911. No clouds. No wind. Just the hard light of judgment. Bert Delige stood stiff and silent in a black suit, the same color as the rope above him. In the yard of the Bellefonte jail, the scaffold groaned under his weight as the noose was cinched tight. He didn't speak. Didn't cry. The clock struck 10:17 a.m.

The trapdoor dropped.

He didn't die quickly.

Delige's body twitched and strained against the rope for over half an hour.

Thirty-seven minutes passed before they finally cut him down and called it done. However, there were those who claimed his neck never broke.

That his eyes were still moving long after the drop. That the rope creaked like something was trying to climb back up.

He was hanged for what he did to Hulda Baudis.

The Widow's Death

She was 51, a widow, returning home through the fields from Scotia on October 16, 1910. She never made it to her door. Her body was found just past a fence line near her house.

Her throat had been cut so deeply she was nearly decapitated.

The earth was torn around her—claw marks in the dirt, blood soaked into the roots.

Delige had known her. He once worked for her husband, running a traveling merry-go-round. That man had taken his own life just two months earlier. And now the last of that household was left cold in the field, staring at the sky.

When asked why he did it, Delige said only that he'd been drinking.

That he didn't remember.

That something came over him.

The Boy with the Bullet

Bert Delige should've been hanged years earlier.

On October 20, 1905, he was walking out for a hunt when a 13-year-old boy named Ralph Williams called out to him from the schoolyard. "Hold on—I want to tell you something!"

The boy jogged up with a grin on his face. Delige turned, lowered his shotgun, and pulled the trigger.

Whether it was a joke, a mistake, or something far worse, no one ever knew. But the blast tore through the boy's calf. Ralph bled out enroute to the hospital aboard Main Line Express No. 1. Delige was arrested—but walked free.

People said he had a bad temper. That his moods turned black. That something in his face went blank when he got the urge.

They should have seen what was coming.

Something Still Walks in the Barrens

Scotia is gone now. The coal seams dried up, and the families drifted off. But the land stayed behind. Locals call it the Scotia Barrens, a patch of twisted woods and scrub flats that stretches through State Game Land 176.

That's where Delige lived. Where Hulda died.

Where something still walks.

In 1977, a man and his friends were hiking through the Barrens when a figure emerged from the trees. Not walking. Gliding. Blacker than the night it came from, tall and featureless, it hovered at the edge of the trail for nearly five minutes. Then it was gone.

The man told the story later at a library in Centre County. A historian nearby overheard, and when he pressed for the location, the man showed him. It was the site of the Baudis home. The same fence line where her body was found. The sighting occurred on April 25th. The anniversary of Bert Delige's hanging.

Locals who hunt or hike the Scotia Barrens still talk about it. Not loudly—and not often—but the stories are there. A black figure seen just beyond the tree line. Tall. Motionless. Watching. It appears in early spring, near the anniversary of Delige's death. Always in the same area—near the remnants of an old fence line barely visible in the brush.

Some claim to have seen it more than once.

Always the same silhouette.

No face.

No sound.

One man swore it kept pace with him for half a mile without making a single footstep. Dogs go stiff in that stretch of trail. Some won't walk it at all.

And every April 25th, someone new comes back with the same story.

If they return at all.

A Bride Lost on the Pike
(Blair/Centre County)

Janesville Pike—Tyrone Area

Janesville Pike, also known as Route 453 (formerly part of old Route 350 before renumbering), threads through a ridge outside Tyrone, where shadows spill across the asphalt and the road itself lures travelers into its grip. The most infamous tale is that of Sylvia—a doomed bride, whose wedding night ended in catastrophe. Her decapitated ghost is glimpsed by unlucky passersby or dissolves into mist.

Always, she wanders the verge in her tattered dress, endlessly seeking her husband, her presence thickening the air with dread.

From *Tyrone Eagle Eye News*, Oct. 27, 2014:

"Drive about nine miles up the Janesville Pike at night. You will first see a few memorials to others killed on the Pike. Just past those memorials, blink your lights on and off eight times. ... If you're (un)lucky enough, you might just see Sylvia in her bloodied wedding dress still searching the ditches along the Pike for her missing husband's corpse."

From *Tyrone Ghost Hunters: Legends of the Janesville Pike*, Oct. 29, 2021: "Arguably the most talked-about ghost story in Tyrone is the legend of "Sylvia," the woman in the white dress that haunts the Janesville Pike."

Slipping Shadows and Vanishing Figures

The Pike harbors more than one ghostly echo. Some speak of a phantom hitchhiker—a girl in vintage clothes who lifts her pale arm, beckoning for a ride, her face a blur in the headlights before she vanishes into the blackness. It's a story told elsewhere, but here the tale festers, rooted in the Pike's history of death and the uneasy silence that follows every passing car.

From *The Pennsylvania Rambler*, Oct. 31, 2021: "Sylvia was the ghost that is said to haunt Route 453, also known as the Janesville Pike... in some versions of the legend, she was decapitated in the accident... her restless spirit wanders the Janesville Pike in search of her missing husband."

Stories That Evolve in Darkness

These legends aren't static—they shift with time and tellers, becoming richer and deeper.

From *Millerverse*, Feb. 15, 2019:

"The cruel darkness of Janesville Pike had existed long before I or Sylvia ever had ... a spirit, tormented by loss, headless in death, to walk the abysmal night of a mountain road that had claimed scores of other lives."

And from *WPSU's "Beware 'Schwaboo': Ghost Tales From Blair County"*, Oct. 31, 2020:

"And one is the ghost of Sylvia that haunts an area that we call 'the pike.' And there are a few of those stories that circulate up and down the mountains of this area of Pennsylvania."

What Hunts at Night

As dusk bleeds into the mountains, Janesville Pike transforms into a snare of shifting light and creeping mist. Headlights jitter over twisted guardrails and the ghostly gleam of memorial flowers. Shadows creep and multiply. Some witnesses have frozen in terror, their flashlights flickering, convinced they saw the bloodstained silhouette of a bride lingering at the shoulder—her empty eyes fixed on them, hollow with grief or hunger, or both.

This is a road that doesn't forgive.

Instead, it absorbs memory and loss, and drips them back into the night, one encounter at a time.

The Bayonets Came at Midnight
(Chester County)

Paoli Battlefield, near Malvern, September 20, 1777

They were asleep when death arrived. Just before midnight, beneath a moonless sky, British troops closed in on the American encampment near Malvern—silent, cold, and without warning. General Anthony Wayne's men, over 2,000 of them, lay in scattered ranks across the open fields. Some had dozed near campfires.

Others curled under coats in the damp grass, their muskets stacked and unloaded.

The order from British command was simple:

No gunfire. No noise. Only steel.

What followed was not a battle. It was a slaughter.

The first bayonets punched through sleeping chests and throats. Men awoke to gurgling screams and blood spraying warm across their faces. Some never had time to stand. Others stumbled up only to be run through, again and again. There were no uniforms in the dark—only shadows, grunts, and the sound of flesh tearing. Those who tried to run were stabbed in the back. Those who begged were finished with boots to the head.

Some men were pinned to the earth like animals, still twitching when the last redcoats moved on.

The Massacre Field

By morning, 53 were dead. Dozens more crawled into the woods, trailing guts and cries behind them. When civilians returned to bury the bodies, they found the fields soaked red, the trees marked with blood spray.

The British never claimed responsibility for the savagery. They called it "a necessary stroke of war." But those who survived called it what it was: *murder.*

They buried the dead in a mass grave, dug in silence. No prayers were spoken.

Something Still Walks There

Today, the Paoli Battlefield lies quiet—but not still.

Paranormal investigators report sudden blasts of freezing air, even in summer.

Lights move low to the ground—like flickering lanterns weaving between the trees.

Some have heard the ragged gasps of dying men, or the desperate slap of bare feet fleeing through wet grass. A few have seen shadows standing where no one should be—motionless, watching from the edge of the tree line.

And some nights, just after midnight, the field fills with sound again.

Not thunder.

Not wind.

Bayonets, finding flesh in the dark.

The Twin Tunnels of Death
(Chester County)

Valley Creek Road, Downingtown
The Woman Who Let Go

They say she came there after dark—alone, walking the rail bed with no lantern. The tunnels cut through the base of a low hill, the creek sliding beside them like a black vein. Sometime around 1900, or maybe later, a woman was seen wandering the track near Valley Creek Road, clutching something in her arms.

A bundle. An infant.

No one ever gave her a name. Only that she'd been left behind—by a man, by a family, or by her own mind.

The story says she climbed into the center tunnel shaft. That she found a beam overhead. That she tied one end of a rope around her neck and the other to a rung and held her child to her chest one last time before she stepped off.

But she didn't fall alone. As the noose tightened, her arms failed. The baby slipped free and plummeted into the darkness below.

There was no scream. No splash. Just silence.

Where the Crying Comes From

Since then, hikers, teenagers, and the curious have stopped in the tunnels at night to see if the stories are true. They park between the arches, kill the headlights, and roll down their windows.

That's when the sound comes.

A slow sobbing echo. Then a high, broken wail—so soft at first you think it's a trick of the wind. But it grows louder. Closer. And if you stay long enough, you'll hear the mother's voice next.

A whisper.

Searching. Begging. Sometimes just behind you.

They say the air grows cold inside the middle tunnel, even in July. That the walls sweat when there's no rain. One girl reported seeing a shape swaying above the tracks, as if suspended from nothing. Another saw a bundle—small, pale, and wet—half-submerged in the creek before it vanished.

The town never officially claimed the legend. But they don't pave the area either. The tunnels are there. The stories come every year.

The Torso in the Creek

In 1995, a fisherman found a suitcase half-buried in the mud near the same stretch of water. Inside was the nude torso of a woman, dismembered, wrapped in plastic and cord. The case had been sealed tight.

Her legs turned up weeks later, 20 miles away. Her head and arms never did.

The police never identified her. No name. No killer. Just another body dumped in a place where ghosts already walk.

What the Locals Say

Stay in the Car

Locals warn visitors now. If you go to the Twin Tunnels, don't walk inside. Don't try to find the crying baby. Don't call out to the woman.

And whatever you do, don't park in the middle and turn off your lights.

Because once the shadows come, they don't always give you back.

Locals in Downingtown remember the stories before the murder, before the documentaries and ghost hunters. Back when it was just a dare between teenagers.

"Kids would drive through and turn their lights off between the two tunnels," one man said. "We all knew not to honk. Not to call out. If you did, you'd hear it."

"The crying," another said. "That baby. I always heard she hanged herself holding it. And if you stop the car, turn off your lights… you'll hear the baby crying."

It's not a ghost story told by strangers.

It's one the town still tells itself.

And the ones who've heard it say it isn't over.

Not while the creek still runs.

Not while the tunnel still sweats.

Not while the baby cries in the dark.

Crybaby Cemetery
(Clarion County)

Saint Luke's Cemetery—Knox

Just southwest of Knox, where the forest begins to fold in on itself, a narrow turnoff from Triangle Road leads to a sloped clearing marked by a sagging fence and moss-covered stones.

Locals call it Saint Luke's Cemetery, but almost no one says that name aloud anymore.

Most just call it Crybaby Cemetery.

The graveyard dates to the 1870s, when death came easily to children and coffins were often the length of a cradle. There are only forty known graves, but the land holds more—unmarked, sunken spots in the grass where names have been lost to rot and silence.

The Twins That Never Slept

For generations, the story has passed in whispers: two infant twins buried at opposite ends of the cemetery, never given a chance to grow or speak. No one remembers their names. No one left flowers. And now, on full moon nights, when the frost clings low and the woods go quiet, the twins begin to cry.

Not loud. Not wailing. Just thin, choked sounds, rising from opposite corners of the cemetery like two voices calling for each other through the dark.

A recurring local belief says if you stay long enough, you may hear not two cries—but three. "The twins cry from opposite ends," said one longtime resident. "But a third one comes from the middle. Close. Too close."

Multiple visitors have noted that the entire cemetery goes silent at dusk. Birds fall quiet. Bugs stop chirping. One account describes hearing a soft whimper—a single child's breath—and then sudden stillness.

"It wasn't wind. It wasn't an animal. It was like something exhaled beside me... and then the whole field went dead quiet."

If you stay long enough, you'll hear both. If you stay too long, you might hear them stop.

Stones That Refuse to Stay Buried

Visitors talk about the cold.

A stillness that presses in. That crawling sensation at the back of the neck—as if someone's standing behind you, just out of reach. Some see shapes between the trees. Some don't make it past the gate.

One grave in particular draws attention: *Henry Cropp, twelve years old.* His marker is a heavy slab with a ball-and-spike ornament affixed to the top—or at least, it's supposed to be.

The stone shifts. Sometimes it falls. Always in the night. Locals have replaced it, bolted it down, even left it untouched just to see what would happen. But by morning, the ball is off. The spike points a new direction. The stone is crooked.

They say Henry doesn't like being forgotten.

Clarion County Commissioner Ed Heasley personally recounted seeing the heavy ball-and-spike headstone on Henry Cropp's grave toppled repeatedly overnight.

"We'd reset it carefully, level and secure. Come back the next morning—down again. No footprints. No damage."

The stone reportedly "falls toward the woods," always the same direction.

What Remains in the Grass

No ghost tours come here. No paved paths or story signs. Just wind, tangled brush, and the graves of children who never stopped mourning.

A visitor once left a small cloth doll between the supposed twin graves after reading about them. Two days later, another visitor found it face-down at the cemetery gate, soaked and scorched at the edges.

"There hadn't been rain. The fabric was damp, but the stone beneath it was dry."

If you go, bring nothing. Leave nothing. Don't step between the twin plots after dark. And if you hear crying from both sides of the cemetery at once—don't move. Don't speak.

They're not calling for you.

But they might *follow* anyway.

Old Stone Holds Secrets
(Clearfield County)

Old Clearfield County Jail – Clearfield Borough, PA

A Jail That Never Let Go

The Old Clearfield County Jail still stands downtown. Built in 1870, it operated over a century, housing murderers, thieves, and the accused who never left. Its thick limestone walls trapped the cold year-round. The gallows once stood behind the building. Solitary confinement meant an underground dirt-floor cell, silent and dark.

It closed in 1983, but it never emptied.

The Second Floor

Inside, cells remain intact. Rust creeps through the bars. The second floor is worst—that's where they kept the violent. That's where people still hear voices.

"I was sitting alone in Cell 17 when I heard someone whisper right behind me," one investigator said. "There was nobody else upstairs."

Another visitor said: "You walk into a cell and feel like someone's already standing there."

The Woman in the Basement

In 1937, a prisoner named Jennie Galley was kept here after being arrested for the hammer murders of her two daughters. She never denied it. Never cried. They moved her later to a state hospital, where she died by her own hand in 1949. But people say she still comes back.

One of the basement cells—the one with the old iron cot—feels colder than the rest. Visitors have heard a woman humming when no one is there. Others report the sharp, metallic clang of a cell door slamming shut behind them. It's not wind. There's no draft in that place.

What Lingers

The jail has hosted investigators and guests. Some leave laughing. Others don't sleep well for weeks. What's felt there isn't loud or obvious. It doesn't scream. It waits.

They don't all say it's haunted.

They say it watches.

Where Pine-Loganton Road Turns Cold
(Clinton County)

The Dancing Cupboard-Pine-Loganton Road–*1879*

Just east of Loganton, Pine-Loganton Road cuts through the forest, barely changed in a hundred years. No lights. No fences. Just trees that lean too close and a wind that doesn't follow the weather. Locals whisper that the road remembers what happened there in 1879. A young servant girl, no older than seventeen, lived in a house along the bend.

A hired hand proposed marriage, but she refused.

Days later, he waited in the trees. When she passed with her bucket, he struck. They found her body two days later, not far from the old stone well. Her name is lost. But the place still carries her.

Those who walk the road at night—especially young men—sometimes see it first in the ditch. A piece of furniture, old, warped, standing upright in the weeds. Then it shifts. Rocks. Dances slowly, as if lifted and set back down by invisible hands. It never appears for women. Only men. And only those walking alone. Some believe it marks the spot where she died—a cupboard from the servant quarters, twisted by grief into a shape her spirit could manage. Others call it a warning. A last attempt to be seen. It is never there in daylight. But the road holds more than one sorrowful memory...

The Garden Ghost

Not far from the bend, Billy Anderson lived alone for over fifty years in the house he inherited from his uncle. He'd once loved a girl. Some say it was the murdered servant. She never returned the feeling.

He built a fence around the house. Planted a garden she would've liked. He never left.

When they found him, he was cold in bed, clutching her faded photograph to his chest. He had been dead for days. The garden had withered. And yet, sometimes—when the moonlight hits just right—you can see him outside. A thin figure in a white suit, pacing between the flower beds that haven't bloomed in decades.

Still waiting for someone who will never come.

Swamp Angel of North Bend
(Clinton County)

North Bend – Young Woman's Creek

North Bend and Young Woman's Creek bear a legend older than the towns themselves. Fascinating early accounts, such as those penned in D. S. Maynard's Historical View of Clinton County (1876), begin as:

"This creek is said to have received its name from the fact that the dead body of a young woman was found at a point where it enters the river.

Others say the Indians scalped and then murdered a young woman there and then threw her body into the creek, hoping it would float off into the river and their act would thus be concealed. A legendary tale is that the Indians there killed a young woman prisoner who could walk no further— that it was a famous and most desirable camping ground— but that ever after this murder, if Indians encamped there at night, her ghost would appear gliding over the surface of the stream, and about the camp and that they were sure to be fired upon by unseen faces if they remained a second night."

There are numerous other legends, but all begin with the chilling statement that the body of a woman—her face pale and drowned, her hair tangled with weeds— was found in the creek.

Some whispered she was slaughtered by shadowed warriors when her legs gave out in the endless forest. Others insisted she slipped beneath the black water, lungs filling with icy silt to escape torment.

Whatever the truth, she did not become a vengeful shade, but something stranger—something mournful. She became the Swamp Angel, a ghost who glides above the black water, her form half-shrouded in fog and trailing with the scent of grave earth.

She could be summoned by those desperate enough to risk her gaze.

Some saw her as a blazing, unnatural fireball; others glimpsed a hollow-eyed woman drifting in the mist, fingers brushing the surface, drawn only to those whose fear was pure.

When Loop Hill Ike Went to the Swamp

One man who dared seek her aid was Isaac Gaines—known in hushed tones as "Loop Hill Ike." A farmer from the forsaken woods of northern Clinton County and a Civil War draft dodger, Ike's name slithered through stories of witches, curses, and things best left unspoken.

In this tale, a witch quarreled with a woman named Maud and spat a curse upon her womb.

The baby, dragged into the world by a midwife named Liz, was born twisted and shriveled—"like a half-grown monkey."

Maud's last, rattling breath left her lips, and her spirit lashed out, haunting Liz with feverish nightmares and cold hands at her throat.

Knowing when the matter clawed beyond even his skill, Ike dragged Liz to the banks of Young Woman's Creek, to the place where the Swamp Angel was rumored to appear. There, beneath a moon smeared with blood, he set foxfire alight for three nights, the rotten glow flickering on their faces as something watched from the trees.

The Ghost's Instructions

On the third night, the Swamp Angel came—her eyes black wells, her voice cold as the grave. She told Liz she must sleep in Maud's fetid bed for three nights, and that only Ike could kill the witch. Liz obeyed, trembling. The ghost hovered at the foot of the bed each night, her presence weighted with sorrow. On the third night, Maud's spirit shrieked and was torn away, never to return.

Killing the Witch

The haunting was ended, but the witch still clung to life. Ike fashioned a crude effigy in her likeness, stuffing it with the venomous weed known as Demon's Delight. He drove a silver bullet through its heart and consigned it to the flames, the fire hissing with a stench like burning hair and blood.

The next day, while Ike visited a local farmer, a deer burst from the underbrush. The farmer fired, missing— but the bullet tore through the wall of the witch's cabin next door.

She collapsed in a shriek, crashing against her cookstove, and the cabin erupted in flames. As the witch's screams faded beneath the roar of fire, Ike watched in silence, letting the farmer believe it was mere accident.

Light Over the Water

Some say the Swamp Angel still appears—a ragged, spectral light drifting through the bone-pale fog over Young Woman's Creek.

She never harms, nor does she linger without cause.

But when called by those who know the old ways, she comes—and when she vanishes, the air grows colder, and the haunting is gone, swallowed by the mist.

Of Hooded Graves and Ghouls
(Columbia County)

Old Mt. Zion Cemetery – near Catawissa

In the 1800s, the freshly buried were not left to rot in peace. They were hunted. Midnight brought more than wind and owls. It dragged with it the shiver of dread— the shuffle of boots across cemetery moss, the clink of spades, the shallow scrape of metal over stone. Grave robbers, ghouls—faces gaunt, eyes wild in lanternlight— prowled the plots where grief still shimmered in the air. They didn't come for flowers or mourning rings.

They came for the bodies: flesh, bone, and all the secrets death tried to keep.

The Ghouls

Beneath the choking stench of turned soil and the ripe musk of death, they wrenched open coffins, wood splintering under their crowbars, not to steal from the dead, but to harvest them. Jewelry was a bonus. The real money came from the meat—limp, bloated, sometimes bursting as they dragged it from the earth's maw.

Medical schools needed cadavers. Dissection tables needed subjects. And when the Anatomy Acts limited legal sources, the schools turned to shadows. Men were paid in secret to deliver fresh corpses—no questions asked. The contractors, in turn, sent their filthiest into the hills with wagons and hooks.

The rules said no private cemeteries. But rules dissolved in the dark, when the dirt was soft and the witnesses were asleep. Robbers would hack at coffin lids, splintering pine and gouging the flesh beneath. They tied a rope around each corpse's neck and dragged it from the box—sometimes in pieces, skin splitting, joints popping, ribs snapping open with a wet crack. The air filled with the squelch of rotting flesh and the reek of putrefaction. They worked fast. No embalming meant the bodies swelled, oozed, and soured within hours. The job had to be done before the rot made the bodies too soft to handle.

What they left behind were mangled caskets, clawed-open graves, and a hole in the world where dignity once was. So, families fought back.

Not with guns. With iron.

The Hooded Graves

Two graves in Old Mount Zion Cemetery near Catawissa bear the scars of that war. Caged in thick metal, riveted to stone, they are not decoration. They are defense. Known today as the *hooded graves*, these rusted contraptions were designed to hold the dead in place. To keep their daughters from being dragged out by the throat.

The names are still visible:

Sarah Ann Boone

Asenath Campbell Thomas

Both died within days of each other in June 1852. Both were young. Both were likely buried after childbirth took its toll. And both were loved enough that someone, perhaps a husband or father or blacksmith brother, forged their cages by hand. Each bar says what the family could not: You will not take them. And no one did.

But the iron remains. A warning. A memory. A grim little riddle in the woods: What kind of dark world needs bars to hold its dead?

The Bloody 32
(Crawford County)

Springboro and Conneaut Lake

They said the trouble began the moment the Erie Railroad put her to work. Engine No. 32—later renumbered 42—lurched through sharp curves and tight turns like a beast with a broken will. Crews whispered what the *Record-Argus* confirmed on December 1, 1896: *"The 'Bloody Engine' No. 32 was involved in another wreck... the tender, two empties and eighteen loaded cars were thrown from the rails at Springboro."*

Engineer Sloss survived with a strained knee.

The Wrecks Begin

In August 1895, she jumped the tracks at Elk Creek near Girard. The *Erie Daily Times* reported she *"made a halt 80 feet down the embankment."*

Engineer Frank Dunbar did not survive.

Another derailment followed near Elk Creek on April 9, 1896.

Renumbered but Not Redeemed

They tried renumbering her to 42, hoping to shake whatever cursed her.

It didn't work.

On August 23, 1900, at Raydure's Curve east of Conneaut Lake Station, *The Evening Republican* recorded: *"Engineer Fred Gilson was instantly killed. Fireman Joseph W. Snedden was hit with escaping steam and badly burned. He died the following day."*

The Hoodoo Reputation

Even after repairs, she turned violent again.

On November 20, 1900, the *Record-Argus* told how she *"jumped the tracks near Greenville and sideswiped a freight train,"* nearly killing the conductor.

By May 26, 1902, the same paper simply called her "the unlucky engine" and reminded readers: *"Three engineers lost their lives on that engine—Beaver, Dunbar and Gilson."*

In October 1902, the *Record-Argus* delivered its final judgment: *"When numbered 32 she killed three men in a short time... Her number was changed, but her disposition remained the same."*

The Tracks She Left Behind

Then she was gone from the timetables. Maybe scrapped. Maybe sent down another line. But the places she broke—Springboro, Raydure's Curve, Elk Creek—still take on a strange quiet at night.

If you stand there long enough, you might feel a vibration through the ground. It starts faint, like a hum in the rails. No whistle. No light. Just the steady approach of something that isn't on the schedule.

She never came back.

But the sound does.

Phantom Plane of South Mountain
(Cumberland County)

Between Dillsburg and Newville

November 18, 1955, began with a heavy, uneasy stillness over the Cumberland Valley.

By afternoon, the first flakes from a brooding winter storm drifted down—an inch in the valleys, but in the ridges of South Mountain, up to eight inches buried the land that night.

The snow swallowed sound and light, muffling the world in unnatural quiet.

Yet the darkness felt alive, each shadow stretching and twitching, as if hiding something restless beneath the drifts. The storm brought more than snow that night—it brought an unease that would haunt the valley, leaving behind questions that gnawed at the edges of sanity.

A Scream in the Sky

Reports poured into Dale Murphy, the county's Civil Defense coordinator. Residents near Newville swore they heard an aircraft in agony, its engines howling in the darkness. Mary Toner, a Civil Defense ground observer, spotted it "flying just above the treetops," its shape cloaked in shadow, before it vanished behind a hill. Seconds later, she heard what she described as "a large explosion"—a sound more like a monstrous roar torn from the earth itself.

Two other observers and numerous citizens also saw or heard it, their voices tinged with fear.

The First Search

Murphy dispatched two Civil Defense planes to the area—no wreckage was found. On foot, more than seventy men combed the Dark Hollow region nine miles southwest of Mount Holly Springs.

The mountains gave up nothing, their ancient woods closing in behind the searchers, swallowing all trace of what had passed through.

The Flares Begin

That night, at 9:45 p.m., the first flare tore through the darkness, an unnatural glow in the black winter sky.

Calls flooded in from Newville residents.

No missing aircraft had been reported to air control.

The next day, searchers returned with air-sea rescue planes from Westover Air Force Base in Massachusetts. Snow hampered the effort; again, nothing was found, as if the mountain itself wished to keep its secrets buried.

A Pattern in the Night

On November 19 at 9:45 p.m., another flare—blood-red this time—ripped through the night.

On November 20, two yellow flares were seen west of Dillsburg in late afternoon, followed by more south of Newville at 6:00 p.m., and another at 9:30. Murphy ordered all fire-truck sirens in the region blown. Fifteen minutes later—9:45 again—a flare arched into the night.

Murphy noticed the timing: "There had to be a meaning behind the flares shooting off at 9:45… but there was no reasoning what the timing meant."

The Green Light

November 21 brought more flares. The first glowed sickly green at 9:45 p.m., followed by three more between 11:00 and 11:30, burning through the darkness like spectral eyes. Later reports whispered that some searchers heard a voice from the mountains—ragged, pleading, not quite human—calling for "Help!"

But the date and location were never confirmed.

The Search Ends

On November 22, Murphy called it off. No wreckage. No survivors. No evidence. That night, for the first time since the initial sighting, no flares appeared.

Asked by reporters what he thought had happened, Murphy gave the only answer anyone could: "It seems to have been a ghost plane. It came out of thin air and vanished into thin air. No one knows where it came from and no one knows where it was going."

The Ridge Still Holds Its Curse

Nearly seventy years later, the ridge between Dillsburg and Newville still carries the same heavy, unnatural quiet in winter. Hunters talk about hearing the distant hum of an engine where no plane flies, and sometimes, the silence feels almost expectant.

No one has found a scrap of metal.

No one has explained the flares.

The snow has long since melted. The questions have not. And on certain cold, moonless nights, some swear the ghost plane still passes low over the ridge—its lights flickering like lost souls, searching for something it can never find.

Ghosts of the Swatara Region
(Dauphin County)

Hummelstown—Fiddler's Elbow on Swatara Creek

The Swatara Region takes its name from the Iroquois and Susquehannock—*"The Place of Eels"* or *"where we feed on eels"*—a reference to the ancient eel weirs once built along the Susquehanna River and its tributaries to catch eels as a source of food. But the waters and hills have carried more than fish. Beneath their surface lies a land haunted by silent graves, unmarked burials, and old paths where the living dare not walk alone.

The Ghost of Chambers Road

Near Chambers Road, in an old cemetery, lies an unmarked grave. From this place, he comes. *"He never leaves his accustomed beat, which leads from the cemetery across the fields to a ravine in the woods. After remaining here an hour or more (no one knows how engaged) he returns by the same route and as he nears the cemetery vanishes away."*

Witnesses agree on his appearance: *"He always appears in his shirt sleeves and with no covering for his head save his thin gray hair."* It is said he can be seen *"any night about twelve o'clock by those from whose eyes the scales have fallen."*

He always returns to the cemetery. Just before reaching the unmarked grave, his body unravels, flesh dissolving into the night air—limbs melting, torso dissipating, and at last his thin gray hair swirling into the hungry dark.

The Headless Wood Chopper

Not all ghosts here belong to churchyards. The "Headless Wood Chopper," said to be the spirit of an early explorer, roams the region freely. As the *Harrisburg Telegraph* noted in the late 1800s: *"He is not always cutting wood, nor does he always carry an axe... He seems to be master of his own movements, and comes and goes when and where he pleases, cuts wood or not as he feels disposed and seems to delight in appearing at odd and unlooked for times and places."*

One encounter, popular in the region in the late 1870s, involved a man traveling from Middletown after dark.

Near a spot known as "Fiddler's Elbow," his horses shied and shuddered. As his eyes adjusted, he saw *"a short man walking beside his team… [who] in a few moments sprang upon the back of the off-wheel horse."* The figure rode there until they reached the edge of the timber, *"when the apparition sprang to the ground on all fours and ran away like a dog."*

The man later insisted no trickery had been played: *"Although it was a cold night, his horses were in a lather of sweat and trembling like leaves, and continued in that state until towards morning."*

A Second Sighting

In 1882, another man returning home late at night was nearly at his door when *"he became conscious of something near him. He looked over his left shoulder and beheld a ghost capering as if in high glee."* Frightened beyond words, he leapt to his door in a single bound. An older man, looking out, recognized the apparition as the Headless Wood Chopper—*"with him both his head and his axe, the former under his arm and the latter upon his shoulder."* This last detail puzzled even the newspaper, noting that it differed from most reports, where the figure was entirely without a head.

The Living Avoid the Paths They Walk

Whether it's the bareheaded ghost pacing back to his grave at midnight, or the headless, grinning fiend leaping onto a traveler's horse, the Swatara Region keeps its dead close. Those who have glimpsed these specters seldom travel alone after dark—the memory of what they saw clings like cold fingers at their throat.

The Ghost of Elizabeth "Harriot" Wilson

(Delaware County)

Edgmont and West Chester Pike

The Crime and the Gallows

In the bitter winter of 1785, Elizabeth Wilson—called "Harriot" by some—stood accused of a crime that curdled the blood: the murder of her own twin infant sons.

The details were whispered in candlelit corners, mothers clutching their babes tighter.

Though the children perished in her care, she wailed her innocence to stone walls and iron bars. But the court was unmoved. In the gloom of January 1786, the sentence was death by hanging. Vice President Charles Biddle, who had penned the pardon, would later confess: *"For my own part, I firmly believed her innocent... The next day when Council met, and we heard of the execution, it gave uneasiness to many of the members, all of whom were against her being executed."*

The Brother's Ride

Her brother, William, haunted by the image of Elizabeth's gaunt face, believed her. In the grip of winter's claws, he rode through black ice and howling wind, each mile echoing with the ghostly cries of lost children. Desperation drove him to Philadelphia, where Governor Benjamin Franklin signed a pardon.

William thundered back across the frozen wastes, frost clawing his beard, the lifeline of his sister's soul pressed to his chest.

Too Late

At the edge of the bleak town green, the gallows loomed like a skeletal finger against the ashen sky. William arrived too late. Elizabeth, pale as moonlight, stood with the noose coiled around her throat. His scream tore through the hush, the pardon fluttering like a wounded bird above the throng.

The hangman did not hear. Or did not care.

The deed was done.

The body twisted; the rope creaked, echoing through the crowd like the closing of a crypt.

The Haunting

They say William's guilt was a wound that never closed, an ache that gnawed through his soul, and Elizabeth's spirit curdled with rage and sorrow. On nights when the cold buries the world, riders in Delaware County glimpse a figure on the back roads—his breath billowing like smoke from the underworld—forever calling out for a pardon damned never to arrive.

Local tradition still warns of her presence: *"The cries of babies can be heard near the intersection of Edgemont and Providence Road... and along Providence Road, some say they have heard the hoof beats and even seen the ghost of William Wilson on his horse in his eternal race."* In the blackest hollows, a woman's wraith lingers at the ragged tree line, her skirts whispering over dead leaves, her eyes hollow and hungry, searching for a salvation that was stolen at the gallows.

It wasn't the wind.

She prowls the woods, restless and vengeful, searching for what was lost. If you meet her gaze in the night, she will follow you home—And you will never be alone in the dark again.

Echoes in the Cellblock
(Elk County)

Elk County Jail — Ridgway

Built in 1872, the Elk County Jail clawed its way from the earth, a grim fortress of stone and iron looming behind the courthouse. Its barred windows and cramped cells confined the desperate and the damned for more than a century. Though the building now hosts county offices and welcomes visitors for tours and community events, its shadows grow long when dusk falls over Ridgway.

Once the last footsteps fade and darkness seeps in, the jail's chilling past stirs, breathing through the corridors like a cold exhalation from the grave.

Echoes in the Cellblock

Former guards, staff, and visitors whisper eerily similar tales—cold spots that slither after you down the corridors, the relentless thud of footsteps echoing overhead when the hallways should be empty, and ghostly murmurs twisting through the darkness, uttered by mouths that no longer exist. In the women's cellblock and solitary confinement, the very air seems to thicken, clawing at your lungs. Some employees, pale-faced and tight-lipped, confess they will not cross the threshold alone after sundown, no matter the reason.

Workers have reported the sound of footsteps echoing in the empty corridors.

They have felt a chill near the old solitary confinement cells.

The Investigations

Paranormal investigators have made the Elk County Jail a regular stop.

They have recorded unexplained noises, temperature drops, and fleeting shadows slipping along the cellblock walls.

A Reputation That Endures

While whispered rumors speak of suicides, madness, and violent deaths behind the jail's iron doors, it is the chilling frequency of recent encounters that sets this place apart from every other haunt in Elk County.

The stories come from law enforcement officers, courthouse workers, veteran tour guides, and the most skeptical of visitors—people who have nothing to gain and every reason to forget what they've seen.

The Elk County Jail endures as the county's most chillingly documented public haunting.

Its stone walls have devoured more than a century of suffering, and on certain nights, that agony claws its way back—icy fingers grazing your skin, sinister eyes glinting from the darkness, and a suffocating certainty that something unseen is watching.

Here, the past refuses to sleep, and the walls themselves seem hungry for more.

Presque Isle's Storm Hag
(Erie County)

Presque Isle State Park— Lake Erie Quadrangle

Presque Isle is a crooked finger of sand curling into Lake Erie, offering a deceptive calm to those who don't know her moods. Beneath the surface, shadows slither between splintered hulls. The lake here is shallow, treacherous, and hungry—a place where fog gnaws at the edges of reality and the water's bed is littered with anywhere from 500 to 3,000 shipwrecks—schooners, fishing craft, passenger steamers.

All were dragged down screaming into what mariners call the Lake Erie Quadrangle, a graveyard deadlier than the Bermuda Triangle.

Early explorers along Pennsylvania's 76 miles of shoreline sought the peninsula's eastern bay as a windbreak during sudden gales. Not all found safety.

And some never stood a chance. Something waited out there in the gloom—something old, patient, and cruel.

The Hag Beneath the Waves

Old Erie mariners speak of a thing in the depths near Presque Isle—a Storm Hag with skin the color of drowned moss and hair like slick green ropes, matted with the bones of fish and men.

Her chin comes to a needle point, her arms long as oars, and her nails curved like fishhooks, dripping with brine.

Her eyes burn yellow in the dark water, moving where no light should reach.

Her teeth are a jagged fence of green, always grinding, always hungry.

As one modern account describes: "This creature is known as The Storm Hag or sometimes called Jenny Greenteeth. She was given this name because her teeth are said to be a deep moss green. Her arms are long with talons, or claws, at the end that drip venom. ... To lure the sailors in she will sing a song, 'The Hag's Song.' The song is short, but is a siren to cast you under a spell to fall in the water with her. She will lurk under the water waiting for the sailors to be drawn closer." — *The Legend of the Storm Hag in Lake Erie, Rocket Reporter*, Jan. 26, 2023—

She waits in the black below, coils of hair drifting like weeds, listening for footsteps and splashes above. When hunger gnaws, she crawls from the depths—sometimes stalking the shore, crouched among twisted trees, her breath reeking of rot, waiting for a stray child to wander too close to the surf.

More often, she calls to sailors. Her voice rides the wind—soft, almost human—before the world turns violent and the storm breaks.

1782: The Last Song

The story most often told is from 1782. A captain, seeing black clouds piling on the horizon, steered hard for Presque Isle's protection. He needed to thread his ship through a stretch of shallows that had wrecked countless others before him.

The storm hit fast. Waves hammered the hull side to side. The crew looked to their captain—men already thinking of their mothers and wives, of graves dug too soon. The captain hesitated, unwilling to risk the reef.

Then, as if the lake itself took pity, the storm fell silent. The clouds thinned to reveal a sheen of moonlight on the bay. Relieved, the captain ordered the ship forward.

Halfway through the shallows, they heard it—a low, coaxing wail, the kind of wind you hear through a nearly closed window. *Come, lads… come. 'Tis safe, it is.*

The moonlight blinked out. Fog rolled in, thick and foamy, followed by the snap of lightning and a crash of thunder that split the sky. The Storm Hag rose—skeletal and immense, slick with slime, eyes blazing like lanterns in the maelstrom.

She wrapped the ship in her squall, shrieking as her long fingers clawed at the rigging, dragging men screaming into the black water.

The lake closed over them, swallowing their terror, as if they had never been.

Mad Anthony Wayne: The General Who Would Not Rest
(Erie County)

Route 322 and Erie County

He was called Blacksnake by Native warriors—because he fought like the serpent, patient, coiled, and merciless when he struck. But among the men he led in the Revolution, he became "Mad Anthony," a name born not from strategy, but from rage, violence, and the mocking curse of a spy named Jemmy the Rover.

Jemmy, jailed in 1781 for disorderly conduct, begged release by boasting of his ties to Wayne. The general refused and sneered: "If you speak of it again, I will order twenty-nine lashes, well laid on." Jemmy spat back: *"Anthony is mad. He must be mad. Mad Anthony Wayne!"* The insult clung like a burr—and the name followed him to his grave.

A Death That Would Not Stay Buried

In 1796, after years of blood and smoke on battlefields, gout ate through Wayne's body at Fort Presque Isle. His flesh rotted from within, the infection devouring him until he died alone in the December cold. He was laid in the earth by the blockhouse at Erie, but death brought no stillness.

Thirteen years later, his son Isaac came to claim him, to bear the corpse home to Radnor. But when the grave was split open, horror spilled out. Wayne's body, not yet decayed, lay blackened and stiff—half-mummified in the frozen clay. To move him whole would be impossible.

So, Isaac did the unthinkable.

A kettle was fetched, great and iron, and Mad Anthony was boiled like swine. The flesh sloughed off in greasy sheets, bubbling in the foul broth until only his bones gleamed pale and naked.

These Isaac packed in a sack. The kettle and flesh were abandoned in the dirt of Erie.

The Scattered Bones of a Mad General

The road home—what is now U.S. 322—was rough, twisting through the wilds of Pennsylvania, flanked by dark forests that seemed to swallow the wagon's lamp.

With every jolt, bones slipped loose from the sack and fell into the dust. A femur here, a rib there, a finger-bone bouncing into the weeds where unseen things waited. Some were lost along the route, scattered, never to be gathered again. They say the land itself grew restless, poisoned by the fragments of a furious soul. His body was split by miles of wilderness—half in a shallow grave at Erie, half strewn like cursed relics across Pennsylvania, the rest laid in Radnor.

But Anthony Wayne was never a man to rest easy.

The Haunting of the Road

They say his ghost still rides the route, stalking the path from Presque Isle to Radnor. Not as a whole figure, but a fractured revenant, dragging its way along the old pike. Sometimes he appears headless, sometimes limping, sometimes with hands clawing at the earth as if to rake up what was lost.

Witnesses have spoken of a soldier in tattered uniform on moonless nights—hollow eyes glowing like embers—searching ditches, pawing the gravel, lifting his lantern over the roadside brush as if hunting for something dropped.

They whisper it is not honor he seeks, nor memory, but his scattered bones—a ghost condemned to wander until every fragment is reclaimed. And if you find yourself on that lonely road, where the dust is deep and the night presses down, listen. You may hear the scrape of something dragging across the stones. A bone, pale and dry, still moving on its own.

Legend of Betty Knox
(Fayette County)

Betty Knox Road — Dunbar / Betty Knox Park

In the last bitter years of the Revolution, Betty Knox lived in the shadow of Kentuck and Tharp knobs. Her mother was long dead, her father a hard settler who taught her to work the fields, haul grain, and drive the ox to the mill in Ferguson Hollow. By the time she was grown, the narrow-rutted road between her farm and the mill was worn deep by her wagon wheels. When her father died, she was left to run the farm alone.

In Union Town, people whispered about her—coming and going without company, eyes downcast. Some swore she was hiding a man: a British deserter she had found half-dead in the woods, whom she nursed to health and kept on her land, safe from the noose. He stayed in the fields while she drove to town.

As *The Morning Herald* (Uniontown, Pennsylvania), February 25, 1925, recorded:

"Isaac Meason built a stone grist mill at Old Union Furnace before the year 1800. Betty Knox, who lived high up on the mountain, was a customer of that mill. She rode an ox, and the path she traveled has since been known as Betty Knox's Road."

The Disappearance

Then, one season, Betty simply disappeared. The mill stones turned in vain without her corn to grind; her stall at market grew cobwebbed and dust-choked. Neighbors found her ox bawling in the barn, eyes wild and rolling, its hide stretched tight over bones that jutted like knives. The fields were a tangle of briar and rot, as if something had clawed its way through the soil. No one had seen her. She was nowhere—gone without a trace between the mill and her farm, as if the earth itself had opened and swallowed her whole.

They called her name for days—searchers fanning out along the creeks and roads, voices echoing under the low, bruised sky: "Betty Knox! Betty Knox!" But there was nothing—no torn scrap of dress snagged on a branch, no trail of spilled grain, not even a smear of blood in the mud. It was as though she had never existed.

The whispers curdled into dread. Some muttered that the Indians had dragged her, shrieking, into the forest where no one would find her bones.

Others imagined a great cat, its jaws painted red, dragging her down into the road's deep cut, her screams muffled by fur and teeth. But the darkest voices insisted it was men—shadows lurking in the brush, who slit her throat from ear to ear for a handful of coins, leaving her to bleed into the black soil, her ghost rooted there forever.

The Bones

Years later, two boys fishing in Tucker Creek stumbled on a grisly relic: a rusted chain snaking into the brush, its end buried in the gnarled roots of an ancient sycamore. There, half-swallowed by earth and rot, lay the yellowed bones of Betty's ox. The chain had worn a deep, unnatural groove in the beast's vertebrae, as if it had strained and choked itself trying to break free.

The tree had grown fat around the links, drinking in whatever horror had happened there. Of Betty, there was no trace—only the hush of the woods, as if they remembered everything.

The Haunting

They say if you stop your car where Betty Knox Road crosses Tucker Creek and runs along Dunbar Creek, you might hear it—the low, mournful bellow of an ox rolling through the mist, fading into the trees.

Or worse: the faint, ragged voice of a man or woman, calling again and again through the dark: *"Betty Knox... Betty Knox..."*

As one account in *Pennsylvania Ghosts and Haunts* puts it: "*Now, if you go to a certain place along the road, you may hear the mournful cry of the ox and hear someone calling, 'Betty Knox! Betty Knox!'*"

But who is calling her name, you might wonder? I thought I'd find out for myself. One gray afternoon, I turned onto Betty Knox Road, parked my jeep, and stepped into the chill. The wind was rising, Dunbar Creek roaring after snowmelt. Ten minutes passed before I heard it—laughter, voices, like a church picnic somewhere in the woods. But there was no one. Then it came, deep and urgent: "*Betty Knox! Betty Knox!*" The call carried on the wind, as if someone with cupped hands was calling for the lost.

It stopped. Then surged again, riding the creek's voice over the rocks. I followed it through laurels and thickets, across deer paths, the sound shifting places every time I drew close. At one point it was so near I was sure I could see the caller through the brush—until it moved, suddenly, to the far side of the creek. My sense of direction is useless, but I made it back to the jeep in record time, heart hammering. I decided I must have imagined it… until two weeks later, telling the story to a friend. "Well, it's a good thing you left," they said.

"Why?"

"Haven't you ever heard of a calling ghost?"

A calling ghost—one that lures you by name, drawing you deeper and deeper until you're too far from help to find your way back. I guess I was lucky. Perhaps Betty and her ox were not.

The Haunted Hickory Creek
(Forest County)

Hickory Creek

Hickory Creek winds through some of the loneliest country in Forest County, its bends hemmed in by dark pines and shrouded hills.

On clear days, the water is slow and glassy, but when the fog rolls in off the Allegheny, the banks feel closer, the woods deeper, and the night heavier.

Locals whisper of strange, ghostly lights that hover above the water—

Pale orbs that drift upstream against the current, sometimes darting between the trees with uncanny intelligence.

They Saw It

On the foggiest nights, voices echo from the darkness, low and indistinct, carrying over the ripple of the creek. "I heard a woman singing just beyond the bend, but there was no one there," claimed one longtime resident in a 1998 interview. Others who live nearby say they've walked the banks alone and heard footsteps pacing them just beyond sight, accompanied by a bone-chilling cold that seeps into the skin.

Some believe these lights and voices belong to the spirits of Native Americans who once lived and hunted along Hickory Creek.

Others claim they are the lingering dead of early settlers—men, women, and children who froze or starved in winters too cruel to outlast.

Whatever their source, the apparitions of Hickory Creek do not linger for company. Witnesses insist the lights vanish the instant you try to follow, and the voices fade like smoke, leaving behind only the rushing water and a deep, gnawing sense of dread. "It felt like something was watching me from the trees," another hiker recounted online. "I left before I could find out what."

The Gray Man of Minister Creek
(Forest County)

Minister Creek—Allegheny National Forest

Minister Creek is a lonely loop of trail, winding through deep hemlock shadows and between sandstone outcrops that glow pale under the moon.

The trailhead lies at the Minister Creek Campground off Route 666, northwest of Tionesta—a place where the night closes in early and silence runs deep.

The deeper you walk into these woods, the more the world seems to fall away, replaced by a haunting sense that something ancient and restless is watching from the trees. Even seasoned hikers have admitted to feeling their nerves fray as dusk falls, the forest swallowing up the last of the light.

The Gray Man

Locals tell of a ghost who walks these woods—a broad-shouldered logger in rough 19th-century work clothes. They call him the Gray Man.

According to the old story, his name was Samuel Harkin, a timberman in the late 1800s. He died when a felled tree twisted against the notch and came back on him, crushing him before his crew could reach him. They buried him on a ridge above the creek. His grave marker is long gone, but his presence is not.

He Returns

Hikers speak of sudden drops in temperature—sharp as if you've stepped from summer into January. Some hear the rhythmic thud of an axe where no one is chopping, followed by the scent of fresh pine sap drifting on still air. Others tell of footsteps pacing behind them on the trail, only to turn and find nothing there.

At night, campers have seen him: a tall, shadowy figure just beyond the firelight, standing silent among the trees. He never comes closer.

He only watches.

The woods seem to hold their breath, and every crackle of the fire feels like it might be answered by a footstep in the dark.

One camper recalled in a 2012 online forum post: "We were sitting around the fire when we saw a man in gray standing near a big pine. He didn't move, just stared at us. When we shined a flashlight, he was gone. The woods were dead quiet, but none of us slept that night."

A hiker in 2007 wrote to the Tionesta Recorder: "I felt like someone was following me the whole way. Every time I stopped, the steps behind me stopped too. At the campsite, my dog started growling at the trees, but there was nothing there—except this awful cold spot. I packed up and left before sunrise."

And when the wind is right, you might hear the slow, deliberate swing of a blade biting into wood—echoing through a forest where even the animals fall silent.

Some say if you follow the sound, you'll find only empty air and an unnatural cold that seeps into your bones, as if the forest itself wants you to forget what you heard.

Mary's Lament
(Franklin County)

Dykeman Pond — Shippensburg

By day, Dykeman Pond in Shippensburg is a picture of calm—its silvered surface unbroken except for the occasional ripple of a duck or a breeze.

But when dusk settles and the fog crawls from the ground, the pond becomes something else entirely.

It is a place where grief lingers, and the past refuses to stay buried.

The Drowning

To the left of the old Dykeman estate, hidden by tangled willow branches and creeping fog, lies the haunted stretch of Dykeman Pond. The locals of Shippensburg know this place is cursed—a place where sorrow festers and refuses to die. For it is here that Mary Dykeman lived and where her life unraveled the moment her child vanished—slipping silently beneath the water, never to return. Neighbors recalled Mary's descent: her eyes hollow, her dress always damp, her hands raw from raking through reeds and muck, searching for a child she would never hold again. Some nights, she'd be seen kneeling at the shore, tearing at her hair, whispering to the black water.

Before long, withered by guilt and sorrow, Mary faded from the world—her body found curled at the waterline, her lips stained blue, her fingers clutching a sodden scrap of fabric.

Mary Returns

But Mary's torment did not end with death. The pond seems to bear a part of her soul. Locals who venture too close after dark speak of an unnatural cold that seeps through their skin, of a suffocating silence broken only by the sound of a woman's voice—hoarse, desperate, echoing through the reeds. Some report glimpsing a gaunt figure, her face twisted in anguish, crawling across the muddy banks, her wet skirts trailing behind her like shrouds. The air fills with a sudden, guttural wail—so raw and inhuman that it turns the strongest legs to jelly and sends even the bravest fleeing for the safety of home.

"It was just after midnight when I heard her—this guttural wailing coming from the reeds. The sound chilled me to the bone, and I swear, I saw a shadowy figure crawling along the water's edge, her face twisted in agony."

—*Local angler*

"Visit Dykeman Pond and you may encounter the ghost of Mary Dykeman still lingering after her baby drowned in the pond in the 1800s. Mary blamed herself for the death of her daughter and died shortly after, still asking where her baby had gone."—*Franklin County Visitors Center*

"Sometimes, when the fog rolls in, you can hear Mary calling for her child. It's the loneliest sound I've ever heard." —*Longtime neighbor*

And still, the legend grows. They say if you follow Mary's voice as it calls from the water, the reeds will part for you, drawing you deeper and deeper until the mud sucks at your boots and the ground turns to ice.

The last thing you might hear is her whisper, closer than you think, desperate for company in her endless search.

If you answer her, you may never leave the pond again.

Death Curve
(Franklin County)

Blue Ridge Summit Route 550 between Pen-Mar and Waynesboro

The twisting stretch of Route 550 between Pen-Mar and Waynesboro winds like a serpent through the Blue Ridge Mountains—a road whispered about in diner booths and gas stations, infamous for its sudden, suffocating fogs and the black ice that creeps in after midnight. Fatal crashes are so common here that the locals have given up counting.

The most notorious spot is a razor-edged bend that the living call "Death Curve," where the dead call home. For generations, travelers have told of a sharply dressed man who materializes in the heart of the night. He wears a suit so black it seems to drink the light, polished shoes untouched by dust, but where his head should be, there is only a void that swallows sound and sense.

Witnesses claim he stands rigid as a corpse at the edge of the pavement—or lurches, headless and silent, into the lane, forcing drivers to wrench the wheel in terror.

When headlights catch him, the figure dissolves with a hiss into mist and shadow, leaving only the echo of a heartbeat skipped in horror.

A Nov. 27, 1920, edition of the *Waynesboro Press* wrote that a headless man walked beside a Waynesboro taxicab driver, then showed up again a few weeks later to two Hagerstown men who described him as "wearing white shoes, dark clothes, and a hat sitting on his shoulder.. ." They saw him both as they reached the curve then again on the other side, while they climbed the hill after crossing the bridge—

Whatever spawned him, his arrival stains the night with dread—the very air thickens, pressing cold hands around your throat. As one survivor muttered, hands shaking on the steering wheel: "When you see him, you feel like the world's gone silent, like the mountain itself is holding its breath."

From PA Oddities ("The Headless Ghost of Waynesboro," Oct. 29, 2023): "...reputed to be the home of a snappily-dressed headless ghost."

Those who have glimpsed his shadow on Death Curve swear, voice trembling, that they will never set tire on that road after dark. As one local put it, "You don't see his face, but you remember his emptiness. It's like looking into the end of everything."

And those who do... ease their foot from the gas as the fog swells around them, curling through the trees like pale fingers. Headlights catch nothing but white, the road vanishing beneath a shroud that presses close and deadens every sound.

Shapes seem to gather in the mist—shapes that keep pace beside the car—and some swear they've seen a figure in fine clothes drifting just ahead, headless, waiting for them to follow.

Things Better Left Unsaid in Sideling Tunnel
(Fulton County)

The Abandoned Pennsylvania Turnpike

Thirteen miles of forsaken pavement lie rotting in the haunted hills of Pennsylvania, where nature claws angrily at the scarred earth.

Skeletal trees loom over the cracked roadway like silent sentinels, their branches twisted into grotesque shapes that blot out the sky.

Grass grows unnaturally thick between the broken slabs, as if something beneath is trying to force its way to the surface. The forest crowds in, hungry, as if desperate to bury every trace of what happened here.

Faded white lines vanish into wild overgrowth, swallowed by creeping shadows. Spray-painted graffiti in sickly greens, bruised purples, and bloody reds stains the concrete, forming symbols that look less like art and more like desperate warnings from those who never escaped.

This is no ordinary road. It is a place where the living are trespassers—an open grave where the past gnaws at your heels.

It is a post-apocalyptic scar, and at its heart festers a tunnel—a mile and a third of blackness so absolute, even light recoils in terror from its maw.

A Highway Born from Abandonment

The roots of this cursed stretch run deeper than bones—back to the late 1800s, when men clawed a railroad through the Alleghenies. Nine tunnels gouged the earth, and with every foot, they unleashed something that should have been left sleeping. The project collapsed, leaving darkness to ferment in the unfinished veins of stone. Only forty percent of the work was finished. The rest lay in ruin.

Nearly fifty years later, during the Great Depression, the Motor Truck Association seized on the abandoned grade. The Pennsylvania Turnpike was born, "America's First Superhighway," with gas plazas, toll booths, and tunnels widened to fit two lanes of cars.

But there was a flaw—one that spilled more than oil.

The east-west tunnels funneled fast, multi-lane traffic down to a single lane. On summer weekends, cars stacked up for hours in the heat and tension. The bottlenecks birthed countless head-on collisions.

Blood stained the asphalt, and twisted metal glittered like bones in the sun.

Sirens howled, but sometimes, when the wind was right, locals swear you could still hear screams long after the bodies were gone.

By the 1960s, the Turnpike Commission cut away three tunnels—Sideling Hill, Rays Hill, and Laurel Mountain—and abandoned the connecting roadway. The Cove Valley Service Plaza was shuttered. The asphalt was left to rot.

A Mile in the Dark

Today, the Southern Alleghenies Conservancy claims the abandoned turnpike. You can hike or bike it—if you have no fear of what waits in the dark. The Sideling Hill Tunnel is 6,782 feet long—long enough for daylight, hope, and sanity to vanish entirely.

When I dared to enter, the tunnel swallowed every sound except the frantic thud of my heart. My headlamp carved a feeble slash through the black—a trembling island of light in a sea of suffocating dark.

Halfway through, the silence became a living thing, pressing against my skull, whispering threats I couldn't quite hear.

The air tasted of rust and old blood.

Something moved with me, just beyond the reach of my light—a hulking shadow, hungry and patient. Every step echoed with the threat of pursuit. Sometimes I thought I saw a flicker in the darkness, a clawed hand or a glint of eyes, but when I swung my light, there was nothing but endless black. My heart pounded so loud I was sure it would call whatever waited there.

I told myself it was a deer, but the darkness felt carnivorous—a living hunger pressing closer with every step.

Whispers in the Black

The tunnel's stories are older than the vines curling across the road outside.

Some say a little girl died here in a car wreck long ago, her spirit forever trapped in the tunnel's icy grip. If you dare toss a pebble into the shadows, you might hear it skitter back to your feet—followed by the cold, childish giggle of someone you cannot see.

Others have seen phantom headlights, cold and spectral, slicing through the black—ghostly vehicles doomed to replay their final moments, screaming out of the dark only to vanish inches from your trembling hands.

But the most feared thing here is not a ghost. Ghosts can be reasoned with, bargained with—or at least understood.

What prowls these tunnels is something older than that.

Something that does not bargain.

It is a hunter.

Witnesses whisper of a Wendigo-like creature, dredged from ancient nightmares—over six feet tall, its gray skin stretched tight over bone, its limbs impossibly long. Its head is a skull with sunken, bottomless eyes that reflect no light, and its mouth splits open far too wide. It moves with a lurching, unnatural gait, as if puppeted by invisible hands, and its hunger is insatiable. They say it hunts the living, feeding on fear before flesh.

They say the Sideling Hill Tunnel is its lair, but the whole stretch of abandoned turnpike belongs to it—the woods, the broken asphalt, and the shadows between every tree.

The Last Glimpse

By the time I reached the far end, my legs were pumping like pistons, my throat raw from the cold air. I stopped, gasping, and turned to look back.

The tunnel mouth yawned behind me—a rotting wound in the hillside, exhaling breath colder than any winter night. The trees seemed to huddle away from it, their branches shivering in silent terror.

Nothing moved. The silence was absolute—so thick it felt like something was holding its breath, waiting for me to let my guard down.

And then—deep in that endless black—something shifted. A shape, impossibly tall and thin, unfurled itself from the gloom, eyes burning with a hunger that froze my blood.

I sped before it stepped into the light, the taste of iron in my mouth and the certainty that if I looked back, I'd never leave those woods alive.

Weeks later, at Harpers Ferry Outfitters, I was thumbing through backpacking gear when I mentioned, almost casually, that I'd biked the old tunnel.

An older man nearby froze.

His eyes narrowed, then found mine.

He stepped closer, voice low and flat, like he was afraid the walls might hear. "If you ever hear it breathe… you're already too close to get away."

I didn't ask how he knew.

Didn't want to. I just swallowed, hardly turned, and nodded dumbly.

Some silences are safer left unbroken—it's better not to speak certain things aloud because doing so could draw unwanted attention from whatever creature or spirit was lurking within that tunnel.

The Ghost of Stovepipe
(Greene County)

Rices Landing – Horseshoe Bend

In 1755, George Washington and his men forded a shallow stretch of the Monongahela to join Braddock against the French and Indians. A little more than thirty years later, John Rice purchased this section of land and founded a community he called Prospect—later renamed Rices Landing.

The riverside town thrived with shops, liveries, and businesses.

The Curve at Horseshoe Bend

Less than a quarter mile from Rices Landing, State Route 1010 plunges steeply and twists into a treacherous, deathly hairpin turn known as Horseshoe Bend. In the early 1900s, a man driving a horse-drawn carriage barreled recklessly into the bend. The horse clung to the path, but the carriage teetered, then violently overturned. The man was hurled through the air—just as the rear wagon wheel slammed down with sickening force, pulverizing his throat and splattering blood across the gravel.

From *Greene County Historical Society archives* (summarized in *The Legend of Stovepipe, Greene County Messenger*, 1970s reprint):

"The wagon wheel mashed his neck so hideously flat the men who found him said it looked 'just like stovepipe'—a grisly, ragged stump spurting dark blood. Soon after, folks passing the bend swore they glimpsed a figure without a head sprawled grotesquely in the weeds, its body twisted in unnatural angles."

His severed head was discovered hours later, its face frozen in a silent scream, rolled down the embankment and tangled in thorny roadside brush, eyes wide and mouth agape as if still reliving the moment of death.

The Name That Brings Him

It wasn't long before travelers began speaking of a headless figure sprawled in the weeds at the bend. Over time, the story became a challenge—those who didn't see him would stop and call three times into the night: *"Stovepipe! Stovepipe! Stovepipe!"*

A local oral history transcript in a 1982 WPA-style folklore collection at the Waynesburg Public Library warns:

"If you were foolish enough to stop at the curve and call 'Stovepipe' three times, you might see him clawing his way up the bank, bloodied hands raking the earth, his ragged neck stump oozing blackness, still hunting for his lost head."

What Waits at the Bend

They say on moonless nights, he still answers— dragging his mutilated body up from the embankment, headless, swaying, and gouging the earth with torn fingers. He prowls the roadside, searching for the head that the wheel stole, and if you linger too long, he might tear you apart, mistaking your face for his own.

Crow Rock Massacre
(Greene County)

Crow Rock Massacre Site — Near Richhill

It was the deceptively warm morning of May 1, 1791, when four daughters of Jacob Crow—Christina (7), Susanna (18), Catherine (6), and Elisabeth (20, married)—set out toward Crabapple Hollow along the Dunkard Fork of Wheeling Creek. Spring had coaxed smiles onto their faces, a fragile shield against the gnawing dread that something monstrous watched from the shadows between the trees.

They played by the water's edge, their laughter thin and brittle, collecting stones and wildflowers torn from the muddy banks. Their brother Michael, 21, appeared with a restless horse and invited Christina to ride with him. She refused. The moment he vanished from sight, a chill swept through the glade—danger crawling into the daylight like a living nightmare.

Ambushed by Shadows

Behind a ledge, two Native American men and a white man painted in their colors erupted like phantoms. One blocked the road, musket glinting with menace, while the others snatched the sisters, grip like iron shackles, and dragged them into the tangled undergrowth. The girls, terror clawing at their throats, whispered frantic prayers in German. Elisabeth's voice, trembling yet fierce, urged her sisters to pray for their souls.

The captors had a choice: kill them or kidnap them. Their eyes were vacant, cold as winter graves, as they chose slaughter. Two men pinned the girls' wrists with monstrous strength while the third raised his tomahawk, the blade catching the morning sun—a flash before the carnage began:

Susanna's head was cleft clean off—blood sprayed over the moss, painting the earth in grotesque patterns, staining it darker than midnight. In the chaos, Christina bolted, her bare feet slipping in the gore as she scrambled up a slope. A musket cracked; a bullet tore a burning line across her scalp. Dazed and slick with blood, she cowered behind a jutting rock, forced to watch her sisters butchered below.

Elisabeth staggered to the creek, blood bubbling from wounds that would not close. Her brother Michael—who had passed them earlier that morning while chasing down a stray horse—was among the searchers who found her. She lingered just long enough to whisper, "Michael, why didn't you come sooner?" before her eyes glazed over, haunted by the last images of her sisters.

She died three days later, her body burning with fever, her mind trapped in those final screams.

From Clio's History of Crow Rock:

"The sisters busied themselves by the creek, when three men jumped them from behind. Two were Indians, the third a white man named Spicer... Susanna died almost instantly, Lisbeth crawled to the creek before succumbing to her wounds, and Catherine was struck and killed in the melee."

Two sisters lie buried in that soil. Elisabeth joined them soon after. Christina alone survived—and the trees remember.

The Haunting That Remains

Today, the creek winds past the massacre site, and the air thrums with an unshakable dread.

Visitors report sudden hoofbeats thundering behind them; icy fingers yanking their hair; shadows that coil and slither in the periphery.

Most chilling of all—a full-bodied

Native American apparition, face streaked with blood, stands sentinel on the road, eyes hollow and unblinking, forever watching where innocence was butchered.

A Ghostly Story Told to Me

A man who lived nearby once told me, "I was down at the old swimming hole on the creek—the same place where the girls were murdered. My girlfriend was with me when we heard screams coming from the banks, the sound warped and hollow, as if echoing through a funnel. I turned to look at her, and her mouth was wide open, like she was screaming along too—but no sound came out. The screams were there one moment, and gone the next. My girlfriend just clamped her mouth shut at the same time and said she felt sick, so we left. It lasted only seconds, but it was still daylight, and it was the most terrifying thing I've ever experienced."

These aren't children's tales.

They are echoes—screams caught in the wind, blood memories frozen in time, the horror still seeping into the earth beneath your feet.

Warrior Ridge's Wailing Shadow
(Huntingdon County)

Along Warrior Ridge Road, near Petersburg

If you cross Warrior Ridge at dusk, the forest's silhouette sharpens into the shape of a watcher—something patient, something that doesn't breathe. The trees hush themselves, and in that uneasy silence, you might sense the pulse of old sorrow.

The railroad cut here, where fog claws its way up from the Juniata Valley, is where locals whisper that a woman wanders after dark, her shape flickering in the mist, forever pacing the brittle edge between our world and something hungry.

Her Story

The story says she was a mother, journeying with her infant in a creaking wagon one spring day in the mid-1800s. Rain battered the hills, and a flash flood tore through the valley, wrenching her from the path and from her child. Days later, they found her tangled in driftwood, her arms empty, her mouth frozen in a scream that no one heard. The child was never recovered.

Hunters, anglers, and late-night drivers speak of soft, broken sobs riding the fog—echoes that seep into your bones. Lantern-light cuts only shadows, but sometimes, just beyond the reach of firelight or headlights, a ragged, stain-thin figure stands hunched on the ridge.

She holds something swaddled to her chest, rocking and weeping.

Glance away, and she's gone, as if the mist itself drinks her in.

- Local newspaper, *Huntingdon Daily News*, August 14, 1937: "Several reputable residents have attested to the strange cries and fleeting white figure on Warrior Ridge. None have dared approach."

- In 1962, local teacher Edna Long wrote in a letter to the editor: "It is the most lonesome sound I have ever heard. The weeping chills you to the marrow. I will not walk that road after dusk."

Some say she appears only to the lost and sorrowful—like a mirror of grief. Others say she is searching. Clutching hope that her child will appear from the trees.

But no one answers.

The Crying Woman of Cherry Tree
(Indiana County)

Cherry Tree

Cherry Tree is a small borough in Indiana County, Pennsylvania—a patchwork of empty fields, skeletal trees, and winding roads where daylight never seems to last. Among the locals, a single warning echoes: never drive these roads alone after midnight. Something waits in the mist. A woman in white, her dress torn and streaked with mud, glides silently along the roadside.

The Pale Woman with Hollow Eyes

Her face is pale and hollow, eyes fixed on something far away, her mouth twisted in silent agony. Every night, she returns, clutching a crumpled letter to her chest—the last words from a husband who vanished into the coal mines, never to return. Sometimes she is seen standing in the center of the road, tears cutting lines through the grime on her cheeks. Sometimes she is heard weeping beside the old bridge, her voice ragged and desperate.

Witnesses claim a sudden chill fills the air, headlights flicker, and radios fill with static as she appears. No one knows what happens to those who stop for her. Some say the woods whisper their names for weeks afterward. Others say the unlucky never make it home.

Drivers who stop in blinking confusion say she vanishes before they can speak—leaving only the empty sway of the roadside weeds where she stood.

The roads here are narrow and overgrown, the houses long dark, their windows watching.

And in the air, heavy as damp cloth, clings the coal dust and the bitter reek of a grief that never left.

Punxsutawney Pike — Phantom Stagecoach
(Jefferson County)

Punxsutawney Pike connected Indiana, Pa to Punxsutawney, Pa

The Punxsutawney Pike is an old road that once linked Indiana, Pennsylvania, to the growing settlement of Punxsutawney. In the late 1800s, it was a key route for stagecoaches carrying passengers, freight, and—sometimes—mine payrolls through the forested ridges between the two towns.

The Legend

On certain fog-heavy nights, locals say the Pike holds its breath. That's when the old stagecoach—drawn by a team of black horses—comes thundering down the road. Its swaying lantern casts an unearthly glow, but the rattle of wheels is eerily silent, and the horses' hooves sound hollow, as if striking more than just earth. Some say the air turns icy and the trees begin to sway even when the night is still.

A resident shared this local lore:

"The horses made no sound as they passed, but the coach lanterns glowed like fireflies in the fog. My grandfather swore he saw it once, coming out of the trees, and it vanished right before his eyes."

Most Popular Version

The best-known account describes a late-19th-century robbery involving payroll money for a nearby mine. Accounts differ—some say the coach overturned on a curve, others that it was ambushed by highwaymen. In either case, the driver and at least one passenger were killed.

The killers, if there were any, were never brought to justice. Folklore says their restless spirits—along with the horses—are doomed to replay that fatal ride.

From a 1970s article in the Indiana Gazette:

"Travelers sometimes report a sudden chill and the unmistakable feeling that something unseen just passed them by on the old Punxsutawney Pike."

Sightings

Witnesses claim the coach materializes without warning in rural stretches of the Pike, especially near old stage stops and crossroads. Some report a sudden chill, as if something unseen just rushed past. Others say the vision barrels straight toward them before dissolving into mist that scatters into the tree line. Those who see the coach say they never forget. Even after it vanishes, the feeling of dread lingers long after the road is quiet once more.

From Thomas White's *Ghosts of Southwestern Pennsylvania*: "Old-timers claimed that on misty nights along the Pike, you could hear the clatter of ghostly hooves and catch a glimpse of lantern light swinging in the darkness, only to turn and find nothing there."

Many of the reported phantom coach sightings are said to occur in the rural, wooded stretches between Clymer and Trade City, where the old road still runs in parts. Although most stories place the haunting firmly in Jefferson County, the Pike's historic reach into Indiana County may explain why sightings are sometimes reported there as well.

And so, if you travel the Pike after midnight, remember to watch the tree line and listen for the sound of hooves that never quite reach your ears. Some say if you meet the stagecoach's gaze, you'll carry a piece of its chill with you forever. Travelers who return home safe often find a thin layer of mist on their doorstep, as if the phantom coach paused there, waiting to see if they'd join its endless ride.

The Legend of the Lost Silver Mine and The Ghostly Remains
(Juniata County)

Along the West Branch Susquehanna

They say the land here keeps its own secrets—and sometimes, it keeps more than that. The hills are older than memory, and night falls thick here, muffling sound and swallowing the unwary. In the 1820s, J. T. Groves was camped along the West Branch when four Native men stepped from the timber, their heavy sacks clinking like shackles in the dead silence.

When Groves caught a glimpse inside, silver ore winked in the firelight—raw, bright, and cold as a corpse's hand. The shadows seemed to press closer, as if drawn to the metal's unnatural gleam.

The men claimed it came from deep in the mountains, a place they had worked long before the settlers. But when Groves offered money to be taken there, they refused. They slipped into the night, and the forest swallowed them whole.

The Relentless Search

"There is a tradition that a silver mine was discovered by a party of Indians on the West Branch, and that, after smelting some of the ore, they concealed the locality so effectually that it has never since been found, though many have searched for it."

—*History of the Susquehanna and Juniata Valleys, Pennsylvania (1886)*

Obsessed, Groves prowled the ridges and hollows for years—Birch Island Run, Spruce Run, Little Bougher Run—scraping cryptic symbols into trees, marking rocks, chasing rumors like a man haunted.

But the deeper he searched, the stranger things became: guttural whispers in the gloaming, footprints that vanished in the mist, and a constant sense that something unseen was following him. The trails bent back on themselves.

Landmarks shifted. The woods seemed to turn him around on purpose, as if alive and unwilling to give up what was buried, or eager to claim another soul.

He died without ever finding it. But he wasn't the last.

Lanterns bobbed in the ravines long after midnight, flickering between twisted trunks like phantom eyes. Old maps, stained with sweat and blood, passed from hand to desperate hand.

Some swore they found black stone that didn't belong here, or pulled copper tools from creek beds—only to see them turn pale by morning, as if the earth itself rejected their trespass.

Others spoke of waking to find all their tracks erased overnight, or of hearing distant cries echoing through the trees when the wind was still.

If you're not meant to find it, the forest will ensure you never come back. Some say it hungers for seekers, and that in certain hollows, the silence is the sound of those who never returned.

Mary of Licking Creek
(Juniata County)

Licking Creek – flows through a rural stretch near Mifflintown and Port Royal before eventually joining the Juniata River

Licking Creek slips through Juniata County's shadowed hollows, its banks tangled with roots and the stone walls of ruined farmsteads. In the early 1800s, a young woman named Mary died here—some say by accident, others whisper of darker deeds. The details are lost, but her sorrow stains the water still.

The Haunting

At dusk, fishermen and lone hikers sometimes glimpse a pale figure in white, gliding above the black current. Her dress hangs sodden and torn, trailing behind her as she drifts to the deepest bend, staring with empty eyes into the water's depths. Step too close, and she melts into mist, leaving behind a breath of cold air and the hush of a grief too old to name.

A local historian once shared under low breath:

"Folks say she shows most when the fog rolls in so thick you can't tell water from willow."

No one remembers seeing her come. No one sees her leave.

But when night settles over Licking Creek, the water seems to hold its breath—and the ache she carries seeps into every ripple, until it feels like the current itself is grieving...and waiting. Perhaps, my friend, it waits for you.

The Silent Mourner
(Lackawanna County)

Forest Hill Cemetery — Dunmore

Founded in 1870, Forest Hill is the resting place of Civil War soldiers, local notables, and whole rows of 19th-century graves now sunk and leaning with age.

The oldest section is unnervingly still, the hush pressing on your ears as if someone unseen is keeping watch.

Even in daylight, visitors report a sense of being observed by eyes that never blink.

The Silent Mourner

Visitors have long whispered about a "silent mourner" who appears near the veterans' section—a woman in dark Victorian mourning dress who glides between the graves, placing flowers on headstones that haven't been tended in decades. No one has ever caught her arriving or leaving; she simply materializes, her face hidden beneath a black veil. Groundskeepers, locking up after dusk, report the chilling sensation of being watched and the prickling certainty they are not alone.

Muffled footsteps and hushed voices echo through the stones when the cemetery should be silent.

One groundskeeper swore, *"Her skirt brushed past me and the air went cold—like I'd stepped into a root cellar."*

Others say the grass behind her sometimes shows a line of dampness even on dry days, as if marked by funeral processions long past.

She never looks up, and if you call out, she vanishes into the stones like a wisp of smoke.

Another witness confessed, "I called out to her, and she simply melted into the morning fog."

Soldiers Still Standing Watch

Multiple visitors and groundskeepers claim to have seen men in old-fashioned military uniforms standing between the graves—solid enough to be mistaken for reenactors, until they dissolve into the air when approached.

One early-morning walker recalled, *"He was just standing there... then he wasn't."*

Sounds of the Past

On certain days, especially near Memorial Day, people hear the slow, mournful beat of a drum, the thin call of a bugle, or the rhythm of marching boots echoing between the stones. The sound lingers even when the cemetery is empty, as though unseen soldiers are assembling for roll call.

Signs the Dead Keep Their Own

Locals tell of flags that remain perfectly upright in storms, or flowers on forgotten graves that stay fresh far longer than they should. Some believe the Silent Mourner and the soldier spirits are bound here—guarding, tending, and remembering—long after the living stopped. As one longtime resident put it, "Forest Hill keeps its secrets—and its dead—very close."

The Fulton Opera House
(Lancaster County)

Lancaster: Fulton Opera House

The Fulton Opera House in Lancaster, built in 1852, stands on ground soaked in blood and terror. Before the theater, this site was home to Lancaster's pre-Revolutionary jail.

In 1763, it became the scene of the infamous Paxton Boys massacre, where 14 Conestoga men, women, and children huddled in fear as the mob forced their way inside.

Eyewitness accounts from that time describe the slaughter as merciless—the victims hacked, bludgeoned, and shot to death, their blood pooling on the stone floor. The bodies of the murdered were left lying where they fell, and their cries echoed through the town for days.

The massacre shocked colonial Pennsylvania, leaving behind a stain of horror that refuses to fade.

The Haunting

Actors, stagehands, and night staff have long claimed the Fulton is more than haunted — it is cursed. The most infamous apparition is a tall, shadowy figure glimpsed in the wings or high in the balcony, its face an ashen blur, eyes black and bottomless.

Some say it is one of the murdered Conestogas, doomed to wander the theater for eternity. Cold, unnatural drafts swirl in the cellars, sometimes carrying the stench of old decay. Footsteps echo in the darkness, slow and deliberate, as if someone — or something — is stalking the living. Some have described hearing guttural whispering in a language no one recognizes, believed to be the dying words of the Susquehannock. One performer saw a man in colonial clothes sitting in the audience. When he blinked, it vanished.

Chilling Details

Sometimes visitors catch the smell of smoke or blood in the stairwells, even when the place is empty. Others have felt a hand touch their shoulder. In the trap room beneath the stage—once part of the jail—tools and props are found moved, shattered, or smeared with dust that looks like dried blood.

In the upper balcony, witnesses have seen a pale, contorted face peering from behind the curtains, its mouth twisted in a silent scream. Children's laughter rings through the lobby, but the echoes often dissolve into sobbing or shrieks. Staff refuse to enter the basement alone after dark. Some visitors have fled the theater, swearing they felt invisible hands grasping at their ankles.

If you ever find yourself alone in the Fulton Opera House after midnight, listen carefully.

The footsteps you hear behind you might not belong to the living.

And if you feel a cold, relentless grip tightening around your ankle, don't look back—some spirits here are desperate for company, and they have been waiting in the darkness for centuries.

Ghosts, Mist, and a Hairy Little Apple Thief

(Lancaster County)

Chickies Rock—Columbia

In 1969, a group of teens near Chickies Rock saw something they couldn't explain—a formless, misty form drifting across a moonlit clearing that rippled smoke-like before fading away. People have seen movement in the woods, but when they approach the shadows, they disappear.

Sightings have caused a stir, joining other eerie tales from the area: a ghostly Native American figure wandering the cliffs, a lovelorn couple doomed to roam together, and a phantom railroad worker pacing the tracks long after the trains have gone silent.

But the most famous resident here isn't a ghost at all. It's very much alive... or so the legend says.

The Albatwitch—Lancaster County's four-foot-tall, fur-covered menace—has been stealing apples and startling hikers for generations.

Its name comes from Pennsylvania Dutch for "apple-snitch," a nod to its most famous pastime: raiding picnics at Chickies Rock.

In the 1800s, startled visitors claimed to see the small ape-like creature grab apples right out of their baskets, only to pelt the gnawed cores back at them, almost as if mocking their inability to catch it.

Small but lightning-fast, the Albatwitch is described as dark-haired, monkey-like, and disturbingly quiet when it wants to be.

Some folklorists believe the Susquehannock painted its likeness on their war shields. Algonquin legends speak of a similar hairy trickster called the *Megumoowesoos*.

The sightings aren't just dusty old campfire tales. In April 2024, a man pulling over at Fishing Creek Nature Preserve for a quick roadside stop found himself staring at something he couldn't explain. Standing in his headlights was a stick-thin figure, the size of a child, peeking from behind a tree.

It smelled of wet dog, moved in short, jittery bursts, and made noises "that didn't belong to any animal I've heard."

Researcher Rick Fisher investigated and found small, human-like footprints—eerily similar to tracks he saw back in 2002, when he spotted a hairy figure strolling down Route 23 near Marietta before it simply blinked out of sight.

So, if you're exploring the wooded trails or riverbanks near Chickies Rock, guard your apples well. The Albatwitch might just be watching from the tree line, waiting for the perfect moment to snatch your snack... and your peace of mind.

As the Columbia Borough Historical Society put it during a 2015 presentation, "The legend of the Albatwitch is as much a part of Columbia as the river itself. Old-timers will tell you: don't eat apples near Chickies Rock after dark."

And as one festivalgoer confided to Lancaster Newspapers during Albatwitch Day in 2019, the stories still echo: "If you're quiet in those woods, you'll hear the whistles. My granddad used to say that's the Albatwitch calling to his kin."

The Lady in White-McConnells Mill Covered Bridge

(Lawrence County)

McConnells Mill Covered Bridge, near Ellwood City and New Castle

Built in 1874, the historic McConnells Mill Covered Bridge stretches across Slippery Rock Creek, its narrow, shadow-soaked frame shuddering with every wind.

Iron trusses groan at night, echoing the footsteps of those long dead.

In the 19th and early 20th centuries, the mill and bridge formed the heart of an isolated community, but the creek below—deceptively beautiful by day—became a black maw in flood, its waters swallowing wagons, livestock, and, too often, people with a hunger that never seemed sated.

Old records and oral histories tell of mill workers losing their footing on slick rocks, of children vanishing in the current, and of the occasional horse-and-buggy that plunged into the churning gorge during storms.

One tragedy still clings to the timbers.

The Lady in White

Locals whisper of a mill worker's wife who, on a storm-lashed night in the late 1800s, tore through the rain with a lantern, her cries for her missing child lost to the roar of the creek. Some say they saw her white dress glowing on the banks before she vanished. When the waters receded, her body was found snagged in the roots downstream—her eyes wide and staring. The child was never recovered, and on stormy nights, some say you can hear her desperate pleas echoing through the trees.

The Haunting
- **The Sound of Hooves** — On fog-heavy nights, travelers crossing the bridge report the sharp, hollow clop of horse hooves keeping pace with them—though the bridge lies empty.
- **The Lady in White** — A pale figure, drenched and shivering in a waterlogged gown, glides along the planks, her soaked hair trailing behind. She pauses in the center, head snapping sharply as if she hears a child's cry.

"I swear, she looked right through me," one visitor recounted online. Another wrote, "There was a cold breath on my neck and the feeling that someone was screaming, but I couldn't hear it— just feel it in my bones."

- "We were walking the bridge late at night, and the air suddenly went ice cold, even though it was August. My friend said she saw a white shape at the far end, but when we approached, there was nothing." — *TripAdvisor, 2017*
- "People always say you can hear a woman crying if you visit after midnight. I thought it was just wind, but it sounded like someone was sobbing right next to the bridge." — *HauntedHouses.com*
- "I've lived near the park my whole life. My grandmother used to say never to cross the bridge after dark, or the Lady in White would follow you home." — *Pittsburgh Ghosts blog*
- "I took a photo of the bridge at night and there was a blurry spot near the center, shaped like a person in a long dress. I tried to recreate it, but it never happened again." — *r/GhostStories*
- Unseen Hands — Visitors report a sudden, icy grip at their sleeves or hems, as though a small, desperate hand is trying to pull them back from the edge. One local shared, "It felt like a child was begging me not to leave, but when I turned, no one was there."
- Midnight Lights — A faint lantern glow will sometimes flicker deep inside the bridge, swaying as if carried, before winking out mid-step.

Some say she hums lullabies, the melody a thin, broken wail barely audible over the rush of the creek.

Others insist they've heard her sobbing, calling a name that's lost to time. More than one visitor, returning to their car, has reported hearing footsteps behind them and a voice whispering, "Have you seen my child?"

Even the water falls silent—its rush swallowed in a strange, smothering stillness—as she drifts by. It's as if the creek itself dares not speak her name, holding its breath in terror, lest it draw her gaze. In that dreadful hush, the world feels suspended, waiting for something ancient, sorrowful, and dark to slip between the shadows of the living.

The Phantom Boatman
(Lebanon County)

Union Canal Tunnel—Lebanon

The Union Canal Tunnel is the oldest transportation tunnel in the United States, completed in 1827 to connect the Schuylkill River and the Susquehanna via the Union Canal.

In its heyday, mule-drawn canal boats passed through daily, carrying goods and passengers between Reading and Middletown.

The tunnel's history is stained with tragedy—grisly drownings, boats splintered in the black water, and workers buried alive in sudden cave-ins. Their screams, some say, still echo beneath the stone arch, a chorus of the damned.

The Haunting:

For decades, boaters, canal workers, and shivering late-night trespassers have whispered of a "phantom boatman" who emerges from the swirling mists near the north portal of the tunnel. He's described as tall, gaunt, and soaked to the bone, his face gaunt as a corpse, with hollow, lifeless eyes.

His sodden clothes leave a trail of stagnant water, yet no footsteps sound as he glides closer. Witnesses say he drags a frayed rope or pole, sometimes guiding an invisible, spectral barge into the tunnel's unlit maw. Some claim that if you meet his gaze, you'll hear a gurgling, watery gasp—like a man's final breath beneath dark water.

A former caretaker in the 1950s told a newspaper:

"He came right out of the fog — clear as you are to me. Then he stepped into the tunnel, and I swear I heard the scrape of the pole on the stones, but there wasn't a ripple in the water."

Visitors walking the towpath after dusk have reported the slow, wet slap of phantom hoofbeats where the path is now overgrown, or the strangled creak of a rope being wound around a cleat.

It seems always just out of sight, always accompanied by the sudden drop in temperature.

"Some nights you can hear the clank of chains and the splash of something heavy falling into the canal, even though it's been dry for decades," reported a local historian. The sounds stop dead at the tunnel entrance, as if swallowed by the darkness. Some even claim a pale, swinging lantern drifts through the tunnel at night, bobbing as if carried by unseen hands. The site is locked and abandoned, yet the air around the entrance is thick with the suffocating weight of unseen eyes.

Local Lore:

"My grandfather wouldn't walk past the tunnel after dark. He said he saw a man with 'water running from his eyes' standing by the entrance, staring at him until he ran home." —*A Lebanon County resident, as told to Union Canal Tunnel Park docents*

"The air goes cold and heavy near that tunnel, like something's waiting for you to step inside." —*Mount Gretna Ghost Walk guide*

Folklore ties the ghost to a gruesome accident in the mid-1800s: a boatman, after a night of hard drink and bitter arguments, tumbled into the canal and was crushed against the tunnel wall by his own vessel.

They say the crew heard him scream, a sound quickly cut off by splintering bone and the rush of black water. Though there's no surviving coroner's report, canal families whispered the tale for generations—warning children that the phantom boatman drags the souls of the careless down into the cold, endless dark.

The Blue-eyed Six
(Lebanon County)

Jonestown: A Quiet Town with a Dark Secret

They said you could tell them apart by their eyes—eyes so cold and unnatural, you'd swear they'd seen the other side.

Even in crowds, even in the smoky glow of a lantern, their gaze would find you: unblinking, inhuman, as if something ancient and hungry peered out through those uncanny blue irises.

The Pact of the Six

Six men in Union Township, Lebanon County—Drews, Stichler, Wise, Brandt, Zechman, and Raber—each shared that pale, glacial blue that caught the light like shards of ice. They were not drawn together by kin, but by something far darker: greed, and the promise of easy blood money.

The Murder at Indiantown Creek

By the winter of 1878, Joseph Raber was a worn-out man, shadows already hollowing his cheeks, his spirit brittle as frost. The six swore to care for him, but their hearts were stone, and their minds already counted the payout; they'd purchased life insurance policies, wagering on his death. On a December night thick with fog, they led him to Indiantown Creek. No one heard his final screams. When his body surfaced, waterlogged and twisted, the current seemed to tug him back below—as if the creek itself wanted him hidden. An official verdict of drowning, but the county thrummed with dread: "The devil's work walks among us," murmured an old woman, clutching her shawl tight, her eyes darting to the shadows.

Justice on the Gallows

At the 1879 trial in Lebanon, the sickening truth spilled out like rot. All six were ensnared by their own words and deeds. The gallows stood waiting, black and skeletal, and crowds pressed in, hungry for justice—or perhaps for a sight of something unholy. Four of them swung together on June 7, the ropes creaking as the trapdoor fell.

They say their pale eyes, wide and glassy, never blinked, staring straight into a darkness no living man could comprehend.

Hauntings by the Creek

But the land never forgot. Farmers near Indiantown Gap whispered of a dripping figure on the bank, soaked clothes clinging to wasted limbs, eyes rolling with terror and accusation.

"Horses refuse to cross the bridge at night. They sense something we can't. Some say it's the old man, Raber, searching for someone to hear his last cry."

—Anonymous townsman, as recalled in oral histories

Horses still balk at the bridge after dusk, nostrils flaring at things unseen. Children, trembling, claim they've glimpsed six silhouettes clustered at the water's edge, faces pale as bone, eyes blazing blue in the moonless dark.

The Curse Endures

The water still carries their secret, black and bottomless. On certain nights, when the mist creeps low and the wind dies, a sudden splash echoes from the creek, followed by a throat-tearing scream that chills the marrow. Linger too long, and you'll feel a hand— clammy, desperate—wrap around your wrist, nails biting deep, dragging you toward the hungry current. Some say it's Raber, pleading for mercy; others whisper that it's the Blue-Eyed Six, reaching for another soul to join them beneath the surface.

He never drowned alone.

The Night Comes Quiet
(Lehigh County)

Coplay—Saylor Cement Kilns

They stand like colossal tombstones—nine stone towers, each ninety feet high, blackened from decades of fire. In their prime, the Saylor Kilns breathed smoke and dust into the air, the sound of grinding rock and roaring flames never ceasing. The men who worked here moved among the heat and choking lime, their lungs turning to stone long before their hearts stopped.

Some never walked out.

The Death Fires

David O. Saylor's dream of Portland cement built these kilns between 1892 and 1893, their flames fed by the labor of dozens of men. It was dangerous work—stone slabs collapsing without warning, heavy carts crushing bones, flames licking out from the kiln mouths hot enough to blind. By 1904, when the fires went out, the ground around them had soaked in sweat, blood, and the desperate cries of the dying.

The Haunting

Night settles here like a shroud. Even in the height of summer, a bone-deep chill seeps from the hollow throats of the kilns—a cold that scrapes at your spine and prickles your skin as if you're being watched.

Flickering Lights: Witnesses tell of lantern-glows drifting in and out of the kiln mouths, too high for any living hand to reach, weaving in patterns that defy sense. One local wrote online, "We went out there late one night, and it got so cold my breath fogged up even though it was July. I heard what sounded like footsteps behind us, but when I turned, no one was there." Another visitor whispered, "The lights moved like they were searching—for something, or someone. I couldn't look away, but I was terrified they'd notice me."

Voices in the Dark: Faint shouts echo through the brick cylinders, the clang of a shovel dropped, a scream that is choked off as if by an unseen hand. An urban explorer wrote, "The kilns always creeped me out. One time I saw a shadow move between the towers. I thought it was my friend, but he was standing right next to me."

A local teen recalled, "We heard a man yelling from inside the kiln. It wasn't an echo—it was like he was trapped and begging us to help. We ran and didn't look back."

The Shadow Worker: The most feared is the dark figure in soot-blackened overalls, seen pacing restlessly near the bases of the towers. His face is always hidden, but if you linger too long, his head snaps toward you with unnatural speed.

The Legend of the Kiln Collapse

Old men in Coplay whisper of a collapse that took a worker alive into the fire. They say he screamed until his lungs burned away, and his shadow was seared into the wall. Some claim you can still see a shape—curved spine, outstretched arms—etched faintly into the soot inside Kiln No. 3.

The park is quiet now. Families wander during the day, but as dusk bleeds out and the wind begins to howl between the towers, the air grows heavy and oppressive. Some say it feels like breathing through stone dust, each inhale thick with dread. Even the crickets go silent.

The Murder of "Patchtown" Catherine
(Luzerne County)

Patch Towns Within Luzerne County's Coal Belt

At the turn of the 20th century, Luzerne County was a land of fire and coal dust. Patch towns—rows of company shacks huddled against the blackened hills—were filled with immigrant families who lived and died under the mine whistle's call. Work was brutal, wages scarce, and tempers always just below the surface.

The Blood in the Dust

On September 10, 1897, that tension tore wide open. Hundreds of striking miners, mostly unarmed Slavic immigrants, marched toward Lattimer. Sheriff James Martin and his deputies met them with rifles. The air split with gunfire. Nineteen miners fell dead in the dirt. Dozens more bled where they stood. Newspapers described bodies "strewn like harvest wheat," their blood soaking into coal dust that already smelled of sulfur and iron.

The massacre entered labor history.

But the ground never quieted.

They say the dead still walk the Lattimer Road.

Phantom Marchers

Each September, the anniversary comes with a hush. Then the gravel begins to crunch—boots in perfect rhythm, as if a column of men still trudges toward the town. Lantern lights bob in the mist. Some faces are half-gone, blackened with bullet wounds.

Others look straight at you, their eyes hollow, their mouths frozen mid-cry.

And then, without warning—rifle cracks in the night. Echoes that do not fade.

The Murder of "Patchtown" Catherine

In those same patch towns, another story bled its way into local memory. Catherine—sometimes O'Leary, sometimes Gallagher in retellings—was an Irish immigrant known for her beauty and defiance. Men admired her. Women whispered.

Some said she was too bold, too willing to question mine bosses, too entangled in union talk.

One night, she vanished. Days later, her body was found at the mouth of a coal mine. Her face was beaten past recognition. Her dress was torn and black with coal dust and blood. The killer was never named. Some said a jealous lover. Others swore it was punishment—silencing a woman who knew too much about secret dealings.

Her ghost did not keep quiet.

Miners walking home at night told of a woman's sobs drifting from the tree line. Children claimed to see her shape by abandoned shafts, her pale hands clutching at the air. In Ashley and Avondale, people swore they heard her calling from the ruins—her cries pitched between grief and rage.

A curse, some said, followed.

Fire Beneath the Earth

After Catherine's death, the earth itself seemed to rebel. In 1915, a coal seam beneath Laurel Run ignited. The fire smoldered unseen, eating through tunnels, belching smoke from cracks in the ground. Homes were abandoned. Whole streets vanished.

The fire still burns to this day.

Locals whispered Catherine had set the mines aflame from beyond the grave—that her restless spirit turned coal to fire, that the patch towns would never know peace while her murderer walked free.

To this day, visitors describe strange lights glowing in empty shafts, the acrid smell of smoke on windless nights, and waves of heat rising from the ground as if the dead themselves were breathing beneath their feet.

Catherine Returns

Her cries still carry on fog-heavy nights.

The marchers still tramp toward Lattimer.

And the earth still burns.

Ralston: The Village of Ash and Iron and Ghosts
(Lycoming County)

Ralston-Old Williamsport & Elmira Railroad

Ralston, once a roaring pocket of ironworks, coal, and rail, sits buried deep in northern Lycoming County. In the late 1800s its furnaces glowed red, its mines roared black, and its tracks shrieked with the iron weight of locomotives. But when the mines closed and the blast furnaces stilled, the town sank into silence. The Williamsport & Elmira Railroad rusted in the weeds.

Houses sagged into themselves. Yet silence did not mean peace.

Ralston kept its ghosts.

The Weeping Woman

For generations, railroad men whispered of a figure who haunted the abandoned line—a woman draped in tattered mourning black, her face hidden behind a veil slick with endless tears.

She carried a lantern whose glow was as pale as moonlit bone, and her keening sobs twisted through the gorge like a curse. When her voice rose, even the bravest men shuddered, for it sounded less like grief and more like a warning from the grave.

"Trains crews in the late 19th and early 20th centuries told of *'a figure in mourning clothes, holding a lamp, weeping at the trestle.'*"

When the whistle screamed, she would vanish, dissolving into the night fog. But those who tarried—who dared listen too long—claimed her wails echoed from the mountainside, clawing at their minds.

A chill would settle over Ralston, and before the week was out, it was said that someone in the village would be found dead in their bed, eyes wide with terror as if they'd glimpsed her face in their final hour.

Some whispered she was a miner's widow, crushed by the grief of the Avondale disaster and drawn north along the steel lines.

Others muttered she was something older, a curse welded into the rails themselves.

The Phantom Brakeman

The rails also carry the tale of a man who refused to leave his post. Old-timers in Ralston still talk about a ghostly figure ambling along the tracks—a railroad man who never left his post.

One suffocating, fog-choked night, a brakeman—known for his loyalty and grim humor—was caught beneath the iron coupling of freight cars.

The shriek of tearing flesh and grinding steel echoed through the yard as the train crushed him beyond recognition, his cries drowned by the engine's roar.

When the smoke cleared, his fellow workers crept through the shrouded rails, lanterns trembling in their hands, finding only blood spattered across the ties and a stench lingering in the air.

Since that night, men have glimpsed him: a hulking silhouette pacing the railbeds, head twisted at an unnatural angle, a lantern swinging from his ruined fist.

He moves in silence, signaling through fog that never lifts.

The unlucky few who approach say his lantern bursts into a blood-red glare, and the air fills with the metallic stink of old wounds.

Some flee before he turns; others claim to have seen his mangled face—mouth open in an eternal scream—before he melts into the mist.

Railroad workers at Ralston long whispered of a phantom brakeman who appeared along the disused tracks, swinging a lantern searching for something lost.

The Signs

The Weeping Woman and Phantom Brakeman are seen most often in autumn, when the hills burn red, the river runs black, and the nights choke with mist thick as shrouds. It is then that the veil between worlds thins and the dead become restless.

The Weeping Woman foretells death; the Brakeman, disaster.

On nights when the wind dies, villagers once swore they heard the thunder of a ghost train barreling through Ralston's gorge—the shriek of its whistle and the echo of phantom wheels on rusted rails.

Yet the line had been dead for decades, and only shadows answer the call.

The tracks are rusted, the mines are sealed. But the dead still ride. And hopefully, they are not looking for you.

The Haunted Kinzua Bridge
(McKean County)

Mount Jewett—Kinzua Bridge

The Kinzua Bridge once stretched across the valley like an iron spine, hailed in 1882 as the "Eighth Wonder of the World." Towering over the ravine, it carried coal and passenger trains on steel legs that groaned under their weight. But in July of 2003, a tornado twisted through the valley and tore much of it down in less than half a minute, leaving only mangled ribs of steel and the collapsed wreckage below.

Most come now for the Skywalk—six hundred feet out onto the surviving span, a glass floor hanging above the rusted carcass of the fallen towers. But some leave with more than just photographs. Locals have whispered for decades about what happens here after dusk. They tell of a sudden, unnatural chill settling over the steel, the wind rising to a low and mournful howl, and then the strangeness begins: a distant, rhythmic clatter, like wheels on rails. The air vibrates, and the unmistakable blast of a train whistle echoes through the hollows, growing impossibly close.

As one visitor later described, "We were up at the bridge near sunset when all of a sudden, we heard a long, lonely whistle echo through the valley. There hasn't been a train through here in years, but we all heard it plain as day. Gave us chills."

Some say you can feel a rush of cold wind as the invisible locomotive passes by, and a few have even claimed to glimpse shadowy shapes moving through the mist, as if the spirits of the bridge's past—workers, passengers, engineers—are still making their final crossing. When the echoes finally fade, the bridge is silent again, but for those who've heard the ghost train, that silence is the most haunting sound of all.

The Bridge Took Lives

During its construction, men fell from the high towers. Some were crushed outright.

Others vanished into the creek bed below. Hikers claim their shadows still wander the girders and railbeds, figures blacker than the night itself.

Cold spots bloom suddenly along the Skywalk, as if someone unseen is standing close.

Kinzua Bridge Ghost Train

"We heard the whistle blow clear as day, but there wasn't a train for miles. Even the ranger said he's heard it, too."

— *Local visitor, as recounted in regional folklore circles*

It wasn't only the bridge that broke.

They say the dead never left. And they never will.

The Lady with the Lantern
(Mercer County)

Beil Hill Road, Greenville — 1880

They used to come in wagons and on foot, just to wait in the dark. Locals. Travelers. The curious and the dared. All of them stood along the stretch called Beil Hill Road, staring into the black along the fence row—watching for the lantern to move. The story they told was always the same. A woman, traveling home by buggy from her sister's late one night in 1880, took the hill too sharp. The horse reared. The cart buckled. She didn't scream.

Her neck snapped clean when the buggy collapsed atop her, pinning her against the post rail fence. They found her just before dawn, twisted beneath the splintered frame, her hand still clutching the handle of her lantern. But that's not the part people remember.

The Light That Won't Leave

It started with a farmer. Just a few weeks after she was buried. He was walking his fence line at dusk, heading toward the same bend. The same stretch. He said he saw her standing there—her nightdress streaked with soil and blood, the lantern swaying in her hand. She didn't move. She just stood there, and then slowly sank into the ground like wet rope sliding into the earth. After that, the light kept coming back. First a flicker, then a steady bobbing glow. It floated just above the ground, moving in wide arcs like it was searching for something—or someone.

It Comes for Family

Her sister and brother-in-law tried to ignore the rumors. But one night, walking back from town, they saw it. The light drifted out from the fence row and into the middle of the road—wavering, like it knew them.

It circled. Then rushed them. They ran, but when they looked back, it was gone. They say she only appears to those who carry a weight—regret, guilt, or maybe something worse. Something that needs to be seen.

She still waits by the fence.

The light still moves. And if it turns toward you—run. Because she's not just trying to be seen. She's trying to see you back. And she always finds the ones she's looking for.

Cotter's Hole
(Mifflin County)

Cotter's Hole, Juniata River Valley

The Cotter name first appeared along the Juniata River in 1796, when Aaron Cotter bought land at the bend. His son, Judas Cotter, grew into a trapper, but his reputation was darker than trade and pelts. It was whispered he robbed men on the trail. Others said he slit throats for their packs and left the bodies for the river. No one trusted Judas, but no one dared confront him alone.

When the reckoning came, it was sudden and violent. The woods echoed with savage blows, the wet crack of bone splitting the hush, and the muffled, desperate groans of a man being beaten into silence. Blood soaked the moss and roots.

As Rhonda Kelley wrote in the Lewistown Sentinel (Oct. 2021):

"He was beaten to death, his body weighted down with rocks, and tossed into a deep hole in the river (Cotter's Hole). Fishermen avoided the spot, believing it to be haunted by the evil spirit of Judas Cotter. It was said if one stared into its dark waters, the spirit of Judas would call to you from below."

The Mifflin County Historical Society has repeated the warning plainly:

"The haunted river location where his spirit may dwell became known as Cotter's Hole. Avoid this place at all costs!"

The black pool became a place of dread. A sickly hush clung to it, thick as fog. Even insects seemed to avoid the bank, as if nature itself recoiled from the evil that slept below.

"Fishermen avoided the spot, believing it to be haunted by the evil spirit of Judas Cotter. It was said if one stared into its dark waters, the spirit of Judas would call to you from below."

Travelers swore the water went corpse-still the instant you drew near, ripples freezing as though something ancient and hateful was watching from below.

Sometimes, just beneath the surface, a face would appear—skeletal, slack-jawed, staring upward with endless, empty sockets. More than one man swore a pale, bony hand, long-fingered and jointed like a spider, rose from the black water, clawing for the living, before vanishing back into the depths.

The October Accident, 1880

The story does not end with his death. Kelley's account in the Sentinel preserves it:

"More than 100 years later, in 1880, on an October, full-moon night a young couple was on their way home, traveling by horse and buggy, along the river road near Cotter's Hole. Suddenly, a gust of wind stirred up some dry autumn leaves, spooking their horse. The buggy slid off the road and the couple tumbled down the bank and into the deep water."

The wind tore through the trees, scattering brittle leaves in a rattling storm. Their horse shrieked—a raw, unnatural sound—and lunged sideways. The buggy lurched, wood splintering, iron shrieking against stone as it slid down the embankment and overturned into the black pool of Cotter's Hole. The moonlight sliced through the branches, illuminating the water as a pit of swirling blackness.

The couple hit the water hard, the cold river biting into their lungs like icy fangs. They fought and clawed upward, choking, dragging one another toward the bank. The man reached land first, gasping on his knees, heart pounding in his ears. He turned—just as a hand rose from the surface beside his wife, pale as death, dripping with river slime.

It was not flesh. It was bone—ghastly, dripping and pale in the moonlight. The fingers, twisted and sharp, grasped at her dress, trying to drag her back beneath the surface. Beneath the waterline, the skeletal face of Judas Cotter leered up at him, jaw slack, black water pouring from its mouth, eye sockets hollow and endless.

"Assisting each other, they were almost out of the water when the man observed a bony hand rising out the water, trying to grab their clothing. It is said he saw the skeleton face of Judas, just below the surface. Not wishing to alarm his wife, he kept the apparition to himself, but was sure to never travel the river road again!"

Lewistown Sentinel, quoting local tradition.

He said nothing. Not then. He hauled his wife to the road, both of them soaked, shivering, skin crawling with the memory of icy hands. They fled without looking back, hearts hammering against ribcages, haunted by the certainty that something watched from the river's edge. Only later did he confess what he had seen. And he swore he would never again travel the river road by Cotter's Hole.

The hole still waits, cold and bottomless, hungry for the living.

Judas never left it.

They Call the Jail Haunted
(Monroe County)

Stroudsburg—Old Stone Jail

In the heart of Stroudsburg, the Monroe County seat, stands the Old Stone Jail, built in 1836. Its thick stone walls and iron-barred windows loom like a fortress against the darkness, casting long shadows that seem to move on their own as night falls.

The building exudes a sense of dread, as if it remembers every cry and confession that ever echoed within.

While countless prisoners passed through its cells, one story persists among local historians and preservationists—a tale whispered by those who have dared to walk its shadowed halls after midnight, when the air is thick with fear.

In 1872, a notorious local figure named William "Billy" Preston was arrested for horse theft, a grave crime in rural Pennsylvania. Preston maintained his innocence, claiming he was framed by a rival, but the evidence stacked against him was overwhelming.

Awaiting trial, Preston languished in the damp, suffocating cell, where the air reeked of rot and despair, growing more haunted with every passing night. The stone walls seemed to close in, gnawing at his sanity as cold drafts carried whispers in the dark.

On a night when thunder rattled the ancient stones and lightning clawed at the sky, the jailer making his rounds found a scene that would haunt him forever: Preston had fashioned a noose from his bedsheet and hanged himself in his cell.

The sight was grotesque—his face frozen in terror rather than peace. The tragedy sent a jolt of fear through the town, and rumors spread that Preston had been driven to despair not just by the charges, but by the relentless visitations of a tormented spirit: the ghost of a previous prisoner, whose screams supposedly still echoed through the corridors at night.

After Preston's death, the jail seemed to come alive with terror. Jailers and prisoners alike began to dread the coming of night.

Heavy footsteps echoed in empty corridors, iron keys jangled violently on their hooks, and a spectral figure in ragged 19th-century clothes was seen peering from cell windows—its hollow eyes reflecting every flicker of lightning. The walls would tremble with unearthly moans, and the very air would thicken until it felt impossible to breathe. Especially during thunderstorms, the jail pulsed with a malignant energy, as if the building itself longed to keep its secrets buried.

"I've worked here for fifteen years, and more than once I've heard someone whisper my name when the building was empty," recalls a long-time tour guide. "Sometimes, when I lock up at night, I feel a cold spot right outside Preston's old cell. It's like someone's standing there waiting for the door to open."

Visitors to the jail-turned-museum have their own stories. One guest book entry from 2009 reads: "Felt a hand brush my shoulder in Cell #2. No one else was near me. Gave me chills all the way down my spine."

Another local historian adds, "There's a reason the old jail was called 'haunted' by the night watchmen. They'd hear footsteps and see shadows, and some swore they caught a glimpse of a man in a tattered coat by the window during thunderstorms."

Some said it was Preston, wronged and restless, doomed to walk the jail until his innocence was proven.

The Old Stone Jail stands today as a museum, but its horrors have not faded with time. Visitors claim the air inside is bitterly cold, even on the hottest summer days, and the silence is broken by sudden, chilling drafts.

A faint sound of weeping echoes through the cells. Some guides refuse to linger near Preston's old cell after dark, convinced that the restless horse thief—and perhaps other lost souls—still stalk the stone corridors, hungry for justice or revenge from beyond the grave.

Ghosts of Valley Forge
(Montgomery County)

Valley Forge National Historical Park – King of Prussia

In the winter of 1777–1778, Valley Forge became less a camp and more a tomb.

General George Washington and his ragged army of twelve thousand men shivered through starvation, smallpox, and frostbite.

With no shoes, many bled across the frozen ground, leaving red trails through the snow.

Half-dead huts sagged beneath the weight of hunger and despair. By spring, thousands were gone—buried in shallow, unmarked graves.

The land itself has not forgotten. Dr. Albigence Waldo, a surgeon at Valley Forge, wrote during that winter: *"Poor food—hard lodging—cold weather—fatigue—Nasty Cloaths—nasty Cookery—Vomit half my time—smoke out of my senses—the Devil's in it—I can't endure it—Why are we sent here to starve and freeze…"* His words echo the depth of suffering that lingers in the air.

Hauntings of the Encampment

The battlefields of Valley Forge were not marked by musket fire and glory, but by silence, sickness, and waiting for death. That silence lingers.

Apparitions of Soldiers: At dusk, pale figures in threadbare uniforms drift between the reconstructed huts, their faces gaunt, their eyes hollow. Some vanish as quickly as they appear, as though melting back into the mist.

Phantom Drums and Muskets: Visitors often hear what should be impossible—marching boots across frozen ground, the roll of distant drums, or the crack of muskets in the empty fields. One park ranger recalled: "Sometimes when I lock up at night, I hear what sounds like marching boots on the gravel. I know I'm the only one there."

Campsites Rekindled: Rangers have reported seeing orange sparks and faint flames deep in the woods. The glow of campfires still flickers—but vanishes when approached, leaving only the cold dark.

Unseen Eyes: Travelers speak of a constant unease—an oppressive feeling of being studied by countless eyes that never blink. A visitor once reported, "We heard drums and muffled voices near the old huts, but when we got closer, there was no one—just the wind."

The very air seems to shiver with what remains.

Washington's Headquarters

The stone house that served as Washington's headquarters is one of the park's most active haunts.

Cold Spots & Footsteps: Guests walk into rooms that suddenly drop in temperature, their breath frosting before them even in summer heat. The sound of boots—measured, deliberate—pace across the upstairs floor when no one is there.

The General Himself: A tall figure, hands clasped behind his back, is sometimes seen staring out the window into the black woods. Many swear it is Washington, still watching over his men. His form fades only when you dare to look too long.

Starvation and the Hospital Tents

Here, the army wasted away. Private Joseph Plumb Martin described it: "To see men without clothes to cover their nakedness, without blankets to lie upon, without shoes, by which their marches might be traced by the blood from their feet..."

Groaning Soldiers: After nightfall, faint voices drift across the fields—hoarse, pleading prayers for bread, water, medicine. Visitors stop, straining their ears, yet find nothing but empty air.

Unmarked Graves: Beneath the soil lie thousands whose names were never carved on stone. Hikers describe a crushing heaviness in certain fields, as if a mass of unseen bodies presses upward from beneath their feet.

It is said the ground itself breathes with the weight of the dead.

The Phantom Sentinel

For generations, locals have spoken of the Sentinel Soldier who still guards the frozen lines.

He is tall but skeletal, draped in a tattered uniform, musket clutched to his chest.

His eyes are black pits, his jaw slack as though frozen in death.

Approach him, and he dissolves into the night air, leaving only the echo of boots crunching snow. At Valley Forge, visitors have long spoken of encounters near the reconstructed log huts. One account tells of a lone walker at dusk who noticed a figure step from behind a tree. The man wore what looked like a ragged Continental uniform. For a moment he seemed like a reenactor lingering after hours, but when the witness turned back for a second look, the figure had vanished.

The Screaming Soldier

One of the darkest traditions tells of a boy-soldier assigned to sentry duty who froze in place, his body discovered upright, encased in ice.

On the coldest nights, hikers along the ridges swear they hear it: a shrill, ragged scream tearing through the dark. It rises once, cuts through the wind, then vanishes.

But the sound is no animal, no echo.

It is the scream of a soldier who never left his post.

Valley Forge is more than a historic park—some call it a graveyard without markers, though there are no formal headstones or visible cemeteries. The suffering of thousands has soaked into the earth, and historical accounts confirm that many soldiers died here, often buried in unmarked, shallow graves. At night, the wind rattles the bare trees like bones, carrying with it the faint, desperate moans of men who never left.

Sometimes, visitors stumble over uneven patches of earth—said to mark the spots where bodies were hastily buried, the soil refusing to forget.

The air grows so cold that breath hangs in the darkness, and those who linger swear they hear shivering voices begging for warmth that will never come.

And some say, if you stand long enough in the night woods, the army still surrounds you.

The Weeping Ghost of Washingtonville

(Montour County)

Katy's Church—Washingtonville

On a lonely hill outside Washingtonville, Montour County, stands St. Peter's Lutheran Church, known to nearly everyone as *Katy's Church*. It is a quiet, rural place by day—weathered stone, a graveyard crowded with leaning markers, and the hum of wind through the surrounding fields. But at night, the churchyard is spoken of in whispers, for it is said to belong to a ghost.

The Legend

Local tradition tells of Katy Van Alen (sometimes spelled Van Allen), a young woman whose life ended violently in the mid-1800s. Some say she was murdered by a jealous suitor; others claim a rejected lover struck her down near the churchyard itself. Her body rests beneath a marked stone in the cemetery, carved with her true name—Catherine Van Alen. But according to generations of townsfolk, her spirit has never lain still.

They call her the Weeping Ghost of Katy's Church.

Hauntings Reported

Visitors speak of strange happenings around her grave and the old sanctuary:

The Woman in White: Katy is most often seen drifting among the gravestones, clad in a pale dress that glimmers faintly in the dark. Witnesses swear she looks heartbreakingly young, her face streaked with tears.

Weeping & Singing: On certain nights, when the fields are still, a soft sound floats from the church—like a woman crying, or singing a mournful hymn. The building is empty, its doors locked, yet the voice carries on the wind.

Unnatural Cold: Even on heavy summer nights, a chill clings to the cemetery. Those who linger near Katy's marker feel as though someone stands close beside them, their unseen breath turning the air icy.

Lights in the Dark: Flickering orbs of pale light have been caught in photographs around her grave. Some locals say they are lanterns carried by those who once searched for her killer, doomed to wander forever.

The Weight of History

Unlike many ghost tales, Katy's story is anchored by a real grave. Her stone still rises among the others, etched with the name *Catherine Van Alen*. The church itself, founded in the 1800s, has witnessed generations of births, deaths, and sorrows. But it is Katy's legend that endures—passed from one voice to another, a chilling warning of betrayal, violence, and grief that never found peace.

To this day, locals avoid the hilltop after dark.

For those who do not, the night often greets them with a sound that freezes the blood—soft weeping, carrying across the stones, as though Katy herself still mourns in the shadows of her church.

Witchcraft on Hexenkopf Hill
(Northampton County)

Hexenkopf Hill—6 miles south of the city of Easton, near the Village of Raubsville

Hexenkopf Hill—its name carved from German tongue as *"Witch's Head"*—still looms above Easton, Pennsylvania, in Williams Township.

For over two centuries, its rocky crown has been a place whispered of in dread. To the early Pennsylvania Dutch settlers, it was no ordinary hill.

It was cursed ground.

It has long been claimed that there were eyewitness accounts of witches dancing around a tree—hand in hand—before disappearing while chanting:

"Be merry, the fiends are roving now! And death is abroad on the wind... linked dances... sang in deep tones mingled with awful laughter."

A Place of Witchcraft and Fear

William J. Heller, in his *History of Northampton County (1912)*, noted the settlers' belief that Hexenkopf was a site of witches' gatherings. The hill was shunned after dark, its massive boulders said to bear the marks of infernal dances. The Powwow doctors of the region—folk healers who practiced charms and cures—warned neighbors never to trespass on the summit when the moon was full.

One early Northampton County resident remembered:

"It was the witches' playground. Folks said their sabbaths were held on the rocks, and no good Christian dared linger there at night."

The Wandering Woman

Among the many legends, the most chilling is that of the ghostly woman who haunts the slopes. Folklorist Henry W. Shoemaker preserved fragments of the tale in his collections of Pennsylvania supernatural lore.

She was said to be a Powwow woman, skilled in healing but envied and feared.

Local superstition twisted her knowledge into witchcraft.

Some accounts claim she was driven to despair by accusation and hung herself among the rocks. Others say she was murdered outright—her body left upon the hill as a warning.

Since then, her pale form has been reported drifting across the stony summit, her face hidden, hands outstretched as if pleading for justice. Sometimes, witnesses said her eyes glowed a burning red from beneath the shroud, and her mouth gaped open in a silent scream. Farmers described their horses snorting, refusing to pass near the hill. Travelers told of sudden icy winds when the phantom appeared, and some returned home with deep scratches on their arms and necks— marks they claimed were left by invisible hands.

In the late nineteenth century, locals spoke of strange sights on the ledges of Hexenkopf. Farmers told of a pale, womanlike figure moving across the rocks at night, her arms twisting as if in grief. Dogs refused to go near the place, and men who climbed the hill said the hair on their necks rose as they watched her drift through the dark.

Strange Lights and Sounds

The ghost was not the only terror. Throughout the 19th century, people spoke of bluish lights flitting over the boulders and disembodied voices drifting down into the farms below. Some nights, a chorus of whispers would rise from the rocks, promising death to anyone who lingered. The most dreaded sign was the sound of wailing carried on the wind—sometimes joined by a guttural, inhuman laughter that sent children screaming from their beds.

Henry W. Shoemaker recorded that Hexenkopf Rock carried a long reputation as a place of supernatural force. Well into his own lifetime, he found neighbors who insisted the witches had not abandoned the hill, and that their presence could still be felt on its summit.

The Haunted Hill Today

The *White Lady of Hexenkopf*—remains a staple of Easton folklore. Visitors still report strange feelings upon the summit: the sense of being watched, sudden drops of temperature, and shadows moving against the stone. Some have claimed to hear footsteps pacing behind them on windless nights, or to glimpse the outline of clawed hands pressed to the rocks as if trying to escape from within.

There are stories of cameras failing, watches stopping, and an unshakeable dread that lingers long after leaving the hill.

The hill is no mere backdrop for folklore. It is a survivor of Pennsylvania Dutch fears—where healing charms, superstition, and whispered tales of witches have fused into one enduring legend of haunting.

Fort Augusta's Restless Dead
(Northumberland County)

Fort Augustus— Sunbury
A Fortress of Shadows

Where the two branches of the Susquehanna meet, Fort Augusta rose in 1756. Hewn from logs and fear, it loomed above the river, a bulwark against French forces and their Native allies during the French and Indian War. Later, in the Revolution, its powder magazines and barracks brimmed with anxious men, watching the river for enemies who never came.

No battle ever razed it. Yet the fort absorbed the misery of frontier war — disease, hunger, exhaustion, and the unending dread of attack. Soldiers died not in volleys of musket fire, but in fever beds, coughing their last into the damp air of the Susquehanna Valley. Their remains were buried hurriedly in the shadow of the walls, where the earth often gave them back.

The Haunting

Though the fort itself is long gone, the ground remembers—and the dead do not forgive. The Hunter House Museum, part of the Northumberland County Historical Society, now sits where the old stronghold stood. Its basement presses into what once was the fort's powder magazine, a place where shadows seem to move on their own. Visitors whisper of voices hissing through the stone walls, icy drafts that claw at the skin, and the relentless, hollow echo of bootsteps when the building is empty and locked.

Some claim to have glimpsed figures in colonial garb—faces pale and featureless, eyes like smudges of darkness—lurking among the museum's exhibits, their forms wavering at the edge of vision. Others say the air in the basement suffocates with the acrid stench of black powder and the faint, metallic tang of blood, as though the magazines are still stocked and the wounded still bleed, awaiting a siege that never comes.

Restless Watch

The fort never fell, but perhaps that is the cruelest fate: its dead remain trapped in endless vigil, their duty cursed to stretch beyond death.

On nights when the Susquehanna fog slithers up the banks and suffocates the old grounds, locals whisper that you can see them: spectral sentries with hollow eyes, muskets in hand, drifting through the gloom, forever guarding a frontier swallowed by time.

They do not rest.

And when the darkness is thickest, neither will you.

Ghost Rider of Waggoner's Gap
(Perry County)

Waggoneer's Gap— North of Carlisle

Waggoner's Gap cleaves through Blue Mountain like a scar. Wind shrieks through the notch, carrying with it the cries of centuries and the cold breath of the forgotten.

The pass was named for Michael Waggoner, who settled here in the 1700s. Long before his farm took root, it was already a road of blood and hardship—used by waggoners and armies, French and Indian War scouts, and even Civil War troops crossing the ridge.

The path was narrow and treacherous. Wagons tipped and shattered on the stone grades. Horses bolted in terror. Men were crushed, bones ground into the dirt. Not everyone who entered the gap came out alive—and some say, not everyone who died ever truly left.

And not everyone stayed buried. On moonless nights, the ground is said to shudder with restless souls.

The Ghostly Rider

For more than a century, stories have clung to the mountain. A rider without a head, seen racing the moonlight. Teamsters swore they met him on the road— a black horse pounding hard against the stone, its rider urging it forward, only to vanish before their eyes.

Some say he was a military courier ambushed in the French and Indian War, his body dumped among the rocks. Others whisper he was a local farmer, murdered while returning from Carlisle, his killers never found.

But all who saw him agreed: he rode hard, as if bound to a road he could never finish.

Signs of the Haunting

From the mouths of Perry County families came the same chilling fragments, carried down like heirlooms:

The creak and groan of wagon wheels grinding over bare stone, though the road lies empty. A rider's shadow darting across the light of a lantern, though no man or beast is near. The hollow cries of a driver urging horses on, his voice echoing against the cliff face, fading into silence.

One farmer said he would rather sleep in the open field than risk crossing the gap after sundown.

Another swore he heard iron-shod hooves keeping pace beside his wagon in the dark—yet when he dared to look, there was nothing but black air.

The Curse of the Gap

Waggoner's Gap remains a place of wild beauty by day, its boulders stacked like broken teeth above the valley. But at night, when storm winds knife down from the ridges and darkness presses close, the gap transforms into a corridor of fear—where every shadow might be watching, and every gust could carry the whispers of the dead.

The locals never forgot.

They said the gap had claimed too many lives to rest easy.

That a man still rode there, long dead, unable to lay down his burden.

On stormy nights, Waggoner's Gap is not a road through the mountain. It is a road into the past—and the dead ride it still.

The Restless Dead of Washington Square Park
(Philadelphia County)

Washington Square Park—Philadelphia

Washington Square, one of William Penn's original five squares, carries a much darker legacy than its peaceful lawns suggest. From the early 1700s until the 1800s, the square served as a potter's field, receiving the bodies of Philadelphia's poorest citizens, enslaved people, strangers, and the abandoned.

By the Revolutionary War, it became a mass grave for soldiers and victims of pestilence. Today, beneath every footstep, thousands of the dead lie just below the surface, unmarked and unrested. The National Park Service records: *"By the 18th century, it had become a burial ground for poor Philadelphians; American and British soldiers during the British occupation of Philadelphia (1777–78); and victims of yellow fever."*

(NPS – Independence National Historical Park)

Soldiers in the Earth

The square holds thousands of unmarked burials, mostly Revolutionary War soldiers who died of wounds, disease, or imprisonment. Their presence is still marked by the Tomb of the Unknown Revolutionary War Soldier, unveiled in 1957. Locals say that on certain misty nights, the air is thick with the scent of earth and decay, and a chill that seeps through clothing and bone.

The tomb inscription reads:

"In unmarked graves within this square lie thousands of unknown soldiers of Washington's Army who died of wounds and sickness during the Revolutionary War." *(Tomb of the Unknown Soldier, Washington Square)*

Local memory has long held the park as sacred ground. As WHYY observed in July 2016, when Philadelphians gather to watch fireworks, they often stand unknowingly over a Revolutionary War mass grave. National Park Service records — and other historical sources — further note that the ground also holds the remains of yellow fever victims, making Washington Square one of the city's most somber burial sites.

The Watcher of the Dead

With so many restless graves, stories of haunting are inevitable. The most famous legend is of a Quaker woman known as Leah, said to appear after dark, gliding silently through the trees. Park guards and late-night wanderers have reported a figure in plain Quaker dress, face pale and unsmiling, moving as though on watch. One nightwatchman recalled: "I saw her standing under the lamplight, just staring at the ground. When I blinked, she was gone." (Ghost Tour of Philadelphia)

Some say Leah's spirit was a nurse or devout woman who cared for the dying in Philadelphia's times of plague and war. Others believe she is a guardian of the thousands still buried beneath the square—watching to ensure they are not forgotten or disturbed.

Alongside her apparition, visitors speak of cold drafts, mists rising from the ground, footsteps on the gravel when no one walks there, and the uncanny sense of being observed. A park visitor described: "It felt like someone was right behind me, breathing on my neck, but when I turned, there was nothing. The hairs on my arms stood up." (Visit Philadelphia, Ghosts of Washington Square)

A Square of Silence

Once a ground of grief, Washington Square is now a park of remembrance. But for those who walk its paths at night, the silence of the trees and the weight of the graves below bring the past back to life. If you wander through Washington Square after dark, listen for footsteps that don't belong to the living, and be wary—because this is a place where the dead are never truly silent.

Eastern State Pen Ghosts
(Philadelphia County)

Eastern State Penitentiary— Philadelphia

The prison ran until 1971. Decades later, when restoration crews ventured through its collapsed blocks, they whispered of terror: sudden, icy winds that sank through the skin, echoing voices calling names that no one would claim, shadows gliding across ruined corridors even when the lights failed. One worker quit on the spot, claiming he heard chains dragging just behind him, though the hallway was empty.

In the early 1990s, Eastern State's locksmith Gary Johnson reported one of the prison's most unsettling encounters. While working on a lock in Cellblock 4, he suddenly felt an invisible force seize him. He later described seeing twisted, anguished faces forming on the cell walls—one even appearing to beckon him closer. (NPR, 2013)

Capone's Torment

Even during its operation, whispers of haunting circulated. In 1929, Al Capone served time here. Guards and newspapers noted his disturbed nights—crying out for "Jimmy" to leave him alone. Jimmy was James Clark, one of the men gunned down in the St. Valentine's Day Massacre.

The Philadelphia Inquirer (Feb. 1930) recorded his restlessness. Prison lore later tied it to Clark's ghost, a torment that no walls could hold back.

Voices in the Ruins

When the last prisoners were transferred out, Eastern State stood silent, a ruin of iron and stone. But silence did not last.

Former guards who returned to walk its crumbling tiers in the 1970s and 1980s told the Philadelphia Daily News of hearing laughter, whispers, and footsteps echoing down abandoned halls. "Sometimes," one guard recalled, "you'd hear keys jangling and voices arguing in empty cells, like the prisoners never left." Another described it as "like a crowd talking just out of sight."

The prison, it seemed, was still occupied.

The Restless Penitentiary

Today the site is a museum. Tourists walk its long corridors. Yet even in daylight, visitors claim a sensation of being watched from the cells. "The hairs on my arms stood up—like someone was breathing behind me," one visitor wrote in the guest book. At night, stories still spread of figures moving along the tiers—faces glimpsed through empty doorways, only to vanish in shadow. Guides sometimes refuse to lock up alone after dark, swearing they hear their names whispered from empty cells.

Eastern State was meant to break the living.

It has also failed to release the dead.

Tragic Ghosts Along the Shohola Tracks

(Pike County)

Shohola- Shohola Train Tracks

A lagging schedule, a blind curve, and one fatal misstep—on July 15, 1864, a wood-burning steam locomotive carrying Confederate prisoners and Union guards thundered into a head-on collision with a coal train near Shohola. The impact tore both trains apart, leaving the ground soaked in blood and mangled steel.

Survivors described seeing bodies strewn like ragdolls through the wreckage, and the cries of the dying echoed through the woods.

At least 60–72 men perished in the carnage. According to a contemporary report: One Union guard described it as though "the two locomotives were raised high in the air, face-to-face against each other, like giants grappling."

Local civilians rushed to assist the wounded, fashioning makeshift coffins from shattered timbers. The dead—both Union and Confederate—were buried in a hasty, shallow mass grave by the tracks, the earth barely concealing the horror beneath.

Some say the ground itself was tainted by the tragedy. In 1911, their remains were reinterred at Woodlawn National Cemetery in Elmira, New York.

The Whispered Haunting

From the wreck's aftermath an enduring sense of dread grew.

Locals and railroad workers whispered that the valley was cursed, and chilling stories took root:

Old-timers in Shohola would not walk the tracks alone after dark, saying "the cries of the prisoners could still be heard when the river fog rolled in."

A visitor in 2015 wrote:

"The hair on my arms stood straight up. I could hear voices in the trees and felt as if someone was right behind me the whole time." (Find a Grave)

Visitors have heard heavy footsteps crunching on the gravel behind them, but when they turn, nobody is there. Apparitions of gaunt, bloodied men in tattered Civil War uniforms wandering the tracks and woods, especially on fog-choked mornings or the anniversary of the disaster.

Distant, anguished cries, panicked shouts, and the mournful clang of a phantom train bell echo through the night, even when no train approaches.

A suffocating sense of unease, icy blasts of air even in midsummer, and the unmistakable feeling of unseen eyes watching from the trees haunt those who walk the tracks or visit the monument.

These were not fanciful tales but echoes of memory. On certain nights, when the fog drifts heavy through the valley, travelers still say the Shohola tracks belong to the dead.

The Restless Boots of Amandon Baker

(Potter County)

Austin—Forests near Keating Summit

Amandon Baker was no ordinary woodsman. A Civil War veteran hardened by battle and wilderness, he lived near Austin, Potter County, in the late 19th and early 20th centuries. His pride, his obsession, was a pair of high-top boots. Cracked leather, worn soles, but always on his feet—never removed, never surrendered.

When Baker died in the early 1900s, the townsfolk buried him as he had lived, boots laced tight around his legs. But the earth would not keep them. Soon after his burial, the forests near Keating Summit and Austin grew uneasy. Heavy stillness hung in the trees. Old logging roads and shadowed trails bore fresh boot prints by morning—broad, deep, impossible to mistake. They began at no place, ended at no place. Only the dark seemed to claim them.

At night, windows rattled with unseen steps. Men and women lying awake in their cabins shuddered as they heard boots trudging past—slow, deliberate, dragging through mud and gravel. The echo lingered long after the sound should have died. Hunters and loggers told of a tall shape flitting between the trees. Some swore moonlight gleamed on polished leather where no man stood.

One old-timer confessed: "It was the boots I heard—clomping right outside my cabin door. I looked, but nothing was there except the fog and those damned footprints."

The legend endures in the PA Wilds. Even now, locals will not walk the backwoods after dark. They say the boots of Amandon Baker still wander—hunting, pacing, never resting. A soldier buried, but not his march.

Headless Horseman-Route 44
(Potter County)

Cherry Springs State Park—Route 44

Cherry Springs, celebrated today for its star-strewn heavens, was once a place where moonlight revealed horrors too vile to describe. Along the old stagecoach road—today's Route 44—riders whispered of a hellish apparition that shredded the night: a headless horseman, blood spurting from the ragged stump of his neck and sluicing down his tattered coat, riding as if hell itself had spat him out.

Stagecoach travelers in the 1800s swore they saw him—a grotesque figure hunched low in the saddle, reins in one hand, a lantern or, more often, a freshly hacked, dripping limb swinging in the other. He erupted from the darkness without warning, his monstrous steed lathered in sweat and filth, eyes rolling wild. Hooves smashed flesh and bone beneath, flinging blood and bits of broken teeth across the rock-strewn road. By the time you managed a prayer, the rider was gone, devoured by the skeletal pines.

Horses reared and screamed, their eyes rolling in terror.

Men clung to each other, faces ashen, hands bloodied from clutching rosaries, the echo of hoofbeats mingling with distant, unearthly shrieks.

Historical Roots

- The stage route between Coudersport and Jersey Shore cleaved through a wilderness that reeked of rot and old blood. Runaway teams, splintered wagons, and corpses left to bloat and blacken under the sun littered the pike. The Potter Enterprise carried reports so grim they curdled the stomach: travelers found with skulls caved in, limbs twisted at impossible angles, faces frozen in screams, their bodies pitched into the stones like butcher's scraps.

- Locals believed the tragedies summoned the rider—some said he was a murdered traveler, others a coachman decapitated in a runaway wreck.

- WPA folklore workers in the 1930s preserved oral traditions of Potter County that told of "a rider with no head seen on the Coudersport pike." Old-timers swore his galloping was the sound of death coming.

Reported Hauntings

- Travelers spoke of hearing hoofbeats pounding the road when no horse was there. The sound would swell in the night, rattling wagon wheels and terrifying draft animals.

- A 19th-century account recalled: *"The rider was gone before you had time to cross yourself, but the horse's steps stayed in your ears all night."*

- Parents near Cherry Springs warned children not to linger at dusk. "If the road goes quiet," they said, "he comes—down from the timber, without a face, without a head. And once you hear the horse breathe at your shoulder, it's already too late."

The Phantom Breaker Boys
(Schuylkill County)

Shenandoah & Pottsville

In the late 19th and early 20th centuries, the anthracite region was built on the backs of children.

Thousands of breaker boys—some no older than seven—endured endless days in the coal breakers, their hands shredded to the bone by slate and their lungs blackened with dust. "Breaker boys" were children forced to labor in the coal breakers—vast, dust-choked buildings where raw coal thundered down chutes.

Perched on narrow wooden planks, they spent endless hours clawing slate and stone from the rushing black stream with bare hands. The air was thick with grit, their fingers torn and bloodied, and many never escaped injury—or the breaker at all. It was brutal, dangerous work. Many of these boys suffered mangled hands, lost limbs, or slow death from coal dust in their lungs.

The machinery didn't just maim; it devoured.

Boys lost fingers, limbs, even their lives.

Some were crushed, sometimes pulled screaming into the gears, their blood turning the coal slick and black.

When the breakers finally closed, the grinding of the machines ceased. But the silence was never complete.

The dead, it seemed, would not rest.

Their Cries Were Heard

From the 1930s through the WPA folklore project, locals told of ghastly encounters at abandoned breakers near Shenandoah and Pottsville. Men passing at dusk shivered at the sound of raspy laughter echoing from the dark, or the scraping of tiny, unseen feet across splintered coal chutes. Some fled after glimpsing pale, coal-streaked faces peering from shattered windows, or after finding fresh, bloody handprints smeared in the coal dust—prints far too recent to belong to the living.

A WPA fieldworker recorded one man's tremulous account: "You could hear them wailing when the wind cut through the boards, and the men said it was the boys who never came home. Some nights, you'd see the shadows writhing, like they were still trying to claw their way free."

Even now, the stories persist. Urban explorers and locals speak of a cold, suffocating dread—the pounding of phantom footsteps on the stairs, guttural whispers in the rafters, the crushing sense of unseen eyes boring into their backs.

In a county where childhood was mangled and discarded, the dead still claw at the ruins, forever trapped in the black, haunted labyrinths of coal.

The Penns Creek Massacre
(Snyder County)

Selinsgrove—Penns Creek Massacre Site

The Tragedy

In October 1755, during the upheaval of the French and Indian War, settlers along Penn's Creek near present-day Selinsgrove fell victim to one of the earliest and most infamous frontier massacres in Pennsylvania. On October 16, a raiding party of Lenape (Delaware) and Shawnee attacked the isolated cabins. Fourteen settlers were killed and eleven were carried away into captivity.

One contemporary record grimly summarized:

"The Indians killed fourteen, wounded one, and carried away eleven."

The horror spread across the frontier and newspapers reported that "the barbarous Enemy spared neither Age nor Sex, mangling and scalping the unhappy Victims."

Survivors described mutilated bodies and children dragged screaming into the wilderness. The land itself seemed marked by violence.

Haunting Legacy

From this massacre grew a legend that clung to the land like a chill. For decades after, locals along Penn's Creek spoke in hushed voices of phantom cries that pierced the midnight stillness, echoing over the black water.

More than one traveler, caught alone at dusk, claimed to see pale figures drifting between the trees—women clutching silent infants, spectral warriors with hollow eyes vanishing before they could be approached. Even the bravest men avoided the riverbanks after dark, and the sense of being watched never quite faded.

By the early 1800s, Snyder County farmers still reported an unshakable unease. In 1823, a respected farmer named Jacob Spade swore that he and his sons heard, on a fog-laden autumn night, "the sound of women's wailing came down the creek as though from no living throat."

Spade described how their lanterns flickered and their horses refused to cross a certain bend in the creek.

Others recounted seeing cold, blue lights gliding across the water, and one neighbor, Margaret Hess, told the local minister she saw "a procession of shadowy figures" moving silently through the reeds, vanishing as quickly as they appeared. These accounts, relayed in 19th-century local histories, gave the valley a reputation for unquiet spirits.

The Penn's Creek Massacre remains both documented history and lingering legend.

The records preserve the facts; the folklore preserves the dread.

Even now, locals say the land grows cold after sunset, and that some nights, the cries return.

The violence scarred the earth so deeply that, for some, the shadows have never lifted.

Headless Shade of Glades Pike
(Somerset County)

Route 31 (Glades Pike)—Somerset

Along the historic Glades Pike—today's Route 31—tales of a headless phantom have plagued the stretch of road east of Somerset since the 1800s.

According to oral tradition, a traveler was ambushed, viciously murdered, and gruesomely decapitated, his head never found.

His body, mutilated and left to rot, was discarded along the lonely pike, staining its history with blood.

Ever since, passersby have spoken of a spectral figure—tall, headless, and shrouded in the stench of decay—drifting along the roadside or staggering through the fields as if doomed to eternally search for his stolen head. Teamsters of the 19th century shuddered at sudden, unnatural chills and horses that shrieked and reared, eyes rolling white at horrors only they could see.

Modern motorists echo the same dread: a shadowy figure materializing at the roadside, sometimes lurching into headlights, forcing terrified drivers to swerve.

Witnesses agree on one horrifying detail—though the figure has no head, it somehow turns toward them, its neck gaping and raw, as if it still sees with eyes torn away by violence.

For more than a hundred years, the Glades Pike legend has stalked Somerset County folklore—a warning carried in low voices when the wind cuts through the mountains.

They say murder bleeds into the soil. It does not fade.

Some corpses never rest.

Some screams never end.

And those who meet him on the roadside never walk away the same. They carry his dying terror—the last choking breath, the crack of bone, the gush of blood sinking into frozen earth—seared into their dreams and their waking thoughts until the day they die.

The Lady in White
(Sullivan County)

Eagles Mere Lake

Eagles Mere, a resort town in Sullivan County, became famous in the late 19th and early 20th centuries for its pristine mountain lake and elegant hotels.

Yet beneath its tranquil surface, the lake has always been a place of unease.

Old-timers whisper that the water hides secrets, and on certain nights, its stillness feels heavy with dread.

The Ghost Story

One of the most chilling legends is that of the Lady in White, seen gliding eerily across the dark surface of Eagles Mere Lake. Oral traditions, documented in Sullivan County historical records and echoed in early 20th-century newspapers, describe her as the restless ghost of a woman who met a violent, watery end here long before the area's golden resort years.

Fishermen and boaters have shuddered at the sight of a pale, spectral figure rising from the black water on moonlit nights—her soaked dress trailing behind her, hair tangled with lakeweed, her eyes hollow and searching. The air grows icy cold as she drifts closer, her form flickering between mist and shadow, until she vanishes without a sound, leaving only ripples where no wind stirs.

The Aftermath

The legend has become entwined with the identity of Eagles Mere as deeply as its cottages and hotels.

Even in recent years, locals claim to feel a suffocating chill near the water's edge—strange, sudden drafts on summer nights, and unnatural ripples when the lake lies perfectly still.

Most unsettling of all, the feeling of unseen eyes watching from the darkness beyond the shore.

Headless Trackwalker of Susquehanna
(Susquehanna County)

Susquehanna Valley Rail Lines

One autumn night, a young man was thrown out of a gathering and, in his stubbornness, chose the tracks as his shortcut home. The rails were quiet, the ties damp with fog rolling off the Susquehanna. He thought he was alone until a light flickered ahead—a lantern swaying back and forth, slow and deliberate.

But as he drew closer, dread clawed at his insides like icy fingers. The figure holding the lantern wore the coat of a trackwalker, but above the collar gaped only blackness—a void that seemed to swallow the faint moonlight. From that emptiness, a choking cold radiated, numbing the boy's limbs. The lantern swung in its hand, casting grotesque, shifting shadows across the rails. The boy's legs locked in terror, yet he followed, drawn by a force that felt both ancient and merciless, unable to look away as the headless shape glided silently down the line.

The phantom stopped beside a heap of twisted, rusted scrap iron scattered across the tracks—metal that, in the suffocating dark, looked like bones picked clean and left to rot. The boy's heart hammered as he realized too late: the phantom hadn't led him to safety, but straight into death's waiting jaws.

A Grim Warning

When the rails began to hum—a deep, insistent vibration that made his bones ache—he knew a locomotive was coming. Panic surged as he snatched the lantern from the ghost's skeletal grip. The lantern's glow wasn't fire but something colder: a spectral blue light that seemed to drain the warmth from his skin. He waved it frantically, his screams swallowed by the unnatural silence until the oncoming whistle tore through the valley with a banshee's wail.

The train exploded into view, its headlamp glaring like a furious eye, brakes screaming and sparks erupting as the wheels shrieked in protest.

It shuddered to a halt just inches from the twisted metal. Crewmen spilled onto the tracks, searching desperately for the man who had warned them. But all they found was the boy, skin leached of color and eyes wide with terror, clutching a lantern that still glowed with that unnatural, icy light—a flame that burned without fire and would never go out.

The headless trackwalker was gone.

Folklore Legacy

In the years that followed, the story bled through the Susquehanna towns. Some swore the phantom had been a brakeman, his head crushed beneath the very wheels he served. Others whispered it was a switchman torn apart in the couplings. Whoever he was, he did not rest. He walked the ties night after night, lantern swaying like a dying heartbeat, bound to the tracks where his body had been broken perhaps searching for redemption from some misdeed.

And they warned—if his light appeared on the rails, you must never turn away. He hunted for others, convinced they too needed saving. To ignore his summons was to invite ruin—or the devil himself to claim the wandering soul. The lantern was no signal of safety. It was the last flicker of redemption.

The Haunted Vista
(Tioga County)

Anna S. Mine, Wellsboro

High above Wellsboro, on the spine of Rattler Mountain, a scenic overlook gazes down into the valley, but its breathtaking view conceals a dark secret. The ground beneath once housed the Anna S. Mine, a small coal operation carved into the unforgiving mountainside. After the mine closed, local hikers and hunters began to whisper of eerie apparitions in the shadows.

The Anna S. Mine, one of several operated by the Morris Run Coal Mining Company near Morris Run—east of Blossburg and south of Wellsboro—left behind more than scars on the land.

Witnesses spoke of spectral miners emerging from the long-sealed shaft after dusk, lamps glowing like fireflies between the trees. The ghostly figures never spoke, never turned their heads—just trudged in a silent line, doomed to replay their endless shifts. Those who dared linger swore the air grew thick with invisible dust, and that the coppery tang of coal grit settled on their tongues, as if the mine itself breathed out its restless dead.

The Coalfield

The Anna S. was not one of Tioga County's major coalfields, but the dangers were the same. Historical records document mule deaths, roof collapses, and miners lost to rock falls or cave-ins. While there is no record of a mass casualty event, the mine's hardships and accidents became woven into local memory.

Folklorists speculate that the legend thrives because the overlook offers a haunting view of the mine's old wound—a barren scar upon the hillside.

The shaft opening, now choked by brambles, is said to exhale icy drafts after sunset. Locals claim it's the breath of those still trapped below, reaching up to chill the living.

Persistence of the Haunting

The Haunted Vista became a staple of Wellsboro's whispered folklore, fueled by hikers who reported seeing spectral lanterns weaving among the trees.

Some hear the distant ring of picks or the mournful bray of invisible mules, though no living soul could be found on the mountain.

Whether born of memory, imagination, or something more, the Rattler Mountain overlook remains a place where visitors pause uneasily, glancing over their shoulders as night settles.

The Ghost of White Deer Pike
(Union County)

White Deer Pike

On the old White Deer Pike, the road carved through a valley strangled by pine. After dusk, the trees became black pillars, devouring every flicker of lantern light until the forest pressed in—endless, shapeless, and suffocating.

No one with sense dared walk it alone.

But one night, a young man named Silas McKean— sometimes called Daniel in retellings—did.

When he crossed between two ancient, rotting stumps, a sickly glow gathered in the air. At first it squirmed like maggots on putrid flesh, then swelled until it burned the shadows away. The light twisted, writhing, until it dragged itself into the shape of a woman in white.

She stood blocking the road, unmoving. Her face was bone-pale, eyes black and bottomless, her skin stretched too tightly over her skull, gleaming with a waxen sheen. The young man froze, his breath snagged in his throat, limbs shivering with cold that seemed to seep from her. She made no sound. She did not breathe. Her mouth began to open, too wide, and then—

And then, in the blink of an eye, she vanished—leaving only the echo of her open mouth and the crawling sense of something watching from the dark.

The Mark of the Dead

When the light died, the stumps beside him began to bleed. Thick, black sap oozed from the wood like congealed blood, slow and viscous, pooling at his feet with a wet, sucking sound. The smell was sharp and sickly-sweet, clinging to his hands and staining his skin, as if the forest itself were rotting from within.

Aftermath

From that night, Silas McKean was not the same. He wandered back to the stumps night after night, staring into the shadows, waiting for her return. Travelers glimpsed him muttering at nothing, lips twitching as if arguing with some invisible presence. His eyes hollowed, his skin grew gray and thin, as if the ghost had drained his very soul.

He lingered there until death claimed him, refusing to leave the cursed road where the phantom woman bled the trees and gnawed away his mind.

Even now, they say, the pines along White Deer Pike close in so tight at night that the darkness feels alive, and a red stain still leaks from the wood, glistening wet beneath the moon.

It isn't the wind.

Travelers whisper that if you linger too long between those stumps, the air curdles, thick and bitter in your mouth, and a sickly glow grows where the road bends. The longer you watch, the brighter it becomes, until the woman tears herself from the dark. She does not move. She does not blink. And if you meet her gaze, something inside you tears loose—something that shrivels and never returns.

That's why some won't take the Pike after sundown. They know what waits there.

And they know, with a terror they cannot shake, that she is still waiting for someone foolish enough to follow her into the trees—and never come out.

Pithole: The Vanished Oil City
(Venango County)

Pithole—Managed by the Pennsylvania Historical and Museum Commission

Pithole was born of greed and firelight. In 1865, fields that had been farmland sprouted derricks overnight. Within months, the town swelled to nearly 20,000 souls. Hotels, boarding houses, saloons, even a theater and a red-light district appeared almost as fast as the wells.

For a brief, delirious span, it was the center of the oil world.

And then it fell. Banks failed. Wells dried. Fires tore through the clapboard streets. By the early 1870s, Pithole was a shell—its wooden empire collapsing back into the hills of Venango County.

What remains now are paths mowed through fields, tracing where bustling streets once ran. Nothing stands but stone foundations and the marks of vanished lives. Yet those who walk the trails say the air is thick and cold, pressing against their skin like unseen hands.

At dusk, a strange, metallic smell drifts on the wind—oil and smoke, though nothing burns. Some hear footsteps behind them, always just out of sight, or catch glimpses of shadowy figures darting between the ruins. The silence feels predatory, as if the land itself is holding its breath, waiting for something to walk into its path, settle down, and try to tame the land again.

Visitors describe Pithole as restless ground—thick, heavy, and unwilling to let go. The wild frenzy of sudden oil wealth and sudden ruin clings like a sickness. The earth remembers every fire, every collapse, every body left behind.

Those who walk there after dark swear it is not empty at all. They hear the low hum of a city that should be silent, feel eyes fixed on them from streets that no longer exist, as if the dead are waiting for the town to rise again.

And it still hungers for the living. Those who cross its ruins are taken in, ground down like the city itself—chewed to pieces and spit back out, hollow, broken, and marked forever by Pithole's curse.

The Ghostly Grave of Allen Ketlaw—The Unburied Man
(Warren County)

Remote Wooded Area of northern Warren County

Allen Ketlaw was a shadowy recluse haunting the bleak wilds of northern Warren County in the mid-1800s

He was an "unpopular, uncanny man" shunned by all, with neither friend nor kin. When Ketlaw ended his own life with a thunderous musket blast, the community recoiled in superstitious dread.

Religious custom forbade the damned from consecrated ground, and no soul dared let the outcast be interred on their land, fearing a curse would follow.

For five nights, Ketlaw's corpse festered in its coffin, abandoned on the wind-lashed earth as a suffocating sense of unease crept through the township. Dread gnawed at the hearts of all who passed. At last, a single fearful soul—driven more by terror than pity—dragged the coffin to a forsaken, tangled wood where the sun never lingered.

The Grave That Spoke

Under the gnarled, looming elms, as a shallow grave was clawed from the frozen soil and Ketlaw's coffin sank into the earth, a malignant hush choked the air. Then—a voice, ancient and cold as the grave itself, hissed from the shadows: "Dig it deeper." The words slithered through the petrified crowd, icy and sharp, leaving terror etched upon every face.

Panic-stricken, the grave diggers clawed at the earth in frantic silence, exhuming the coffin, burrowing deeper into the dark loam, and burying him anew. They fled the scene, wordless and haunted, as a suffocating dread pressed ever closer.

Ghost or Wind?

Some later claimed it was nothing but the restless wind in the branches. Yet for those who stood among the graves that night, the voice was unmistakable—a spectral command from beneath the earth, demanding the honor and rest denied to the damned. No one who heard it slept soundly again.

Shades of Death
(Washington County)

Shades of Death Road — Near Avella

In its earliest days, travelers named the narrow, shadow-choked road between Bethel Ridge Road and Campbell Drive *Shades of Death*. Hemlocks and gnarled oaks twisted together so thickly overhead that sunlight was blotted out, the world below plunged into a perpetual twilight.

The air reeked of decaying leaves and something coppery, metallic.

Even on the brightest days, chill drafts slithered across travelers' necks, as if invisible fingers were sizing up their throats. Over time, timbering has stripped away some of that darkness, but the road's name—and the dread it inspires—remains, clinging to the place like mold in a forgotten cellar.

The Stagecoach Ambush

Local lore tells of a Pittsburgh–Steubenville stagecoach ambushed here, its wheels screeching to a halt as masked men swarmed out of the fog. The robbers dragged passengers into the blackest tangle, where screams were quickly swallowed by the suffocating woods. They butchered every soul, leaving limbs sprawled at impossible angles, red smears painting the roots. The shades of these slaughtered victims are said to drift along the roadside, their torn mouths gaping in silent wails. When headlights catch them, faces flash with hollow eyes and stained teeth. They leer at passersby, as if plotting vengeance they were never able to take in life.

The Cliftonville Riot Dead

The road's other haunting is tied to the Cliftonville Riot of July 17, 1922. That morning, some 500 union miners marched along the ridge above Cliftonville to halt the work of nonunion men. At about 5:15 a.m., just as the unsuspecting miners below started toward the tipple, the armed union men burst from the woods, charging down into the town. Gunfire cracked and echoed for nearly two hours. By the time it ended, Brooke County Sheriff H.H. Duval and at least thirteen miners lay dead.

The wounded and dying union men were dragged, bleeding trails through the undergrowth, into the suffocating forest a few miles away along Shades of Death Road. Some pleaded for mercy, their voices bubbling with blood, before the darkness swallowed them whole. Those who did not survive were buried in frantic silence, their graves shallow and unmarked, the earth above them disturbed and oozing. Their bodies were never recovered—only the stench of rot and the uneasy silence remained.

Lingering Paranormal Reports

Today, many claim the road is haunted by the riot's dead. After dark, travelers have reported chilling phenomena: the thud of boots pounding through brush, breathless gasps echoing in the blackness, and the crack of phantom gunfire tearing the night. Sometimes, low, guttural groans seep from the tree line, accompanied by the stench of gunpowder and rotting flesh. Some drivers glimpse bloodied figures limping along the shoulder, faces half-missing, hands clawing at the air for help that never comes.

Cars shut off. A ghostly child has been seen in the road, dress soaked.

Some have heard a voice whisper their names from the woods.

An eyewitness, 2007:

"One night, a figure stepped in front of my headlights. He was missing half his face, but he smiled and waved. I turned the car around and never went back."

Some say the spirits are not merely restless—they are furious, doomed to relive the moment their skulls split or bullets tore through their chests.

Their rage twists them into something monstrous, always searching for the men who left them behind.

On moonless nights, they drift along the roads—slow, hollow-eyed, and heavy with dread. Looking for something they left behind years ago. And perhaps, on such a night, they will find it in you.

A Little-bit Haunted Cemetery
(Wayne County)

Philipsburg Cemetery—Philipsburg

Among Wayne County tales preserved by local historians, one of the more haunting whispers through the graves of a cemetery near Philipsburg.

This story is not of rattling chains or shrieking banshees, but of a silent figure—a presence that clings to the night air, lingering like a shadow too patient to fade, too cold to vanish.

The Sightings

Visitors say the graveyard breathes a cold unlike any other, as if the earth itself mourns. The air stills, even when wind claws at the trees beyond the stone walls. And then—among the crooked rows of markers—appears a figure, half-formed in the dimness, where light cannot quite reach.

Always the same: tall, silent, faceless. Its presence presses against the skin, a chill that seeps deeper than the bones. It drifts between the stones, pausing at certain graves as if keeping vigil for secrets only the dead recall. Its gait is measured, heavy, as though treading old pathways long worn into the earth by centuries of sorrow.

Those who linger speak of its unnerving persistence. Leave and return, and it will still be there, pacing slowly, as though the watch has no end. Some locals whisper that the figure is the restless spirit of a grave digger, buried among those he once tended—unable to abandon his eternal duty. Others claim it is a soldier, lost to time, condemned to patrol the dead forever, a sentinel for souls who cannot rest.

Folklore Legacy

The spirit is not violent. Yet its silence unsettles more than any scream.

To see it is to feel the weight of eyes that do not exist, to hear footsteps echoing in the mind where no living thing walks.

Its quiet is a suffocating hush—a presence that fills every shadow and lingers long after sight is gone.

They say if you walk the cemetery at night, it will appear—always just far enough away, always turned toward you, face blank as the moon.

And when you leave, the dread follows: something loyal, something ancient, has marked you with its watchful gaze, and you will feel its presence even after the stones have vanished behind the trees—haunted, perhaps, for as long as you remember.

The Ghosts of the Darr Mine
(Westmoreland County)

Van Meter & Jacobs Creek—Darr Mine

By 1907, the Darr Mine festered like a rotting wound in the hillside above the Youghiogheny River, about thirty miles southeast of Pittsburgh.

Since the 1850s, it had clawed at the earth's bowels, carving tunnels that seeped darkness. Nearly 400 miners toiled there—Germans, Greeks, Poles, Austrians, Hungarians, and Italians—men who had crossed oceans for the promise of a better life.

Instead they found themselves devoured daily by the gaping, greedy maw of the mine for twelve to fourteen hours at a stretch.

Most existed in Van Meter on the same side of the river, or Jacobs Creek on the opposite bank. Each morning, those from Jacobs Creek drifted over the churning, black water on the Sky Ferry cable car, returning late at night, their faces obscured by soot like funeral masks. They murmured always of lurking death: tunnels collapsing, the suffocating embrace of coal dust, and the invisible, explosive reek of methane. Their pleas for more airshafts were swallowed by corporate indifference, leaving them entombed alive by greed.

A December of Death

December 1907 was a month drowned in blood and sorrow. Just weeks before, 362 miners had perished in the Monongah disaster in West Virginia, their bodies heaped in the earth's cold maw. On December 1, the Naomi Mine in Fayette County erupted, claiming thirty-four more souls. Some survivors from Naomi, still marked by ash and grief, found work at Darr. They should have fled from that cursed ground.

The Day of the Explosion

December 19 dawned as any other, deceiving in its ordinariness. The mine had slumbered for two days. Two hundred and forty-nine men and boys descended into its gullet, swallowed by darkness. At 11:30 a.m., a group of miners trespassed into forbidden tunnels, their open-flame cap lamps casting ghastly shadows on the slick walls.

Somewhere in the suffocating gloom, the gas ignited, birthing hellfire.

Newspapers reported that black smoke and fire poured from the mine mouth, the blast strong enough to hurl timbers, coal cars, and even mules into the air. When the choking haze lifted, the valley fell into a heavy stillness—broken only by the cries of women rushing toward the pit mouth. The entire valley convulsed. The earth's breath reeked of charred meat and scorched bone, a stench that clawed at the living and marked the land forever.

The dead lay piled in heaps. Many were burned beyond recognition. Others were headless or limbless, torn apart by the blast. The horrid stench of burning flesh filled the air around the shaft.

Only ten men crawled from the inferno, their eyes haunted, their souls forever scarred by what they had seen below.

The Voices in the Dark

In the days after, searchers swore they heard noises from within the mine—sounds that should not have been there- a strange sound—like the rattle of pick hitting on stone—was heard from deep in the workings after the explosion, though no living man remained inside.

Some insisted the noises were nothing but trapped air or shifting timbers.

Others whispered it was the restless dead, condemned to labor in darkness for eternity, their pickaxes tolling a requiem beneath the earth.

The Trapper Boy

One ghost story took root quickly. Ardo Shupe of Smithton told it as it was told to him by a young trapper boy. His job was to open trap doors underground in complete darkness to let coal cars pass, miles from daylight. One evening, the boy felt someone walking beside him in the black. Terrified, he ran home and vowed never to go back. His father, angry, told him ghosts were foolishness and threatened to thrash him if he refused to work.

Two days later, the mine was closed. On the morning of December 19, the boy nearly stepped through the entrance when a wave of dread stopped him cold. He turned and fled home, bracing for a beating that never came. The explosion killed his father and every man on his shift. The boy had been saved—by something unseen.

The Feast of St. Nicholas

That same day, hundreds of Orthodox Christian miners refused to work so they could attend the Feast of St. Nicholas at the Jacobs Creek Carpatho-Russian Orthodox Church across the river. The boss threatened to fire them.

They went anyway. While they prayed, the mine blew apart.

Their devotion had saved their lives. In gratitude, they built St. Nicholas Orthodox Church in Jacobs Creek and St. Nicholas Byzantine Catholic Church in Perryopolis—memorials to the protector who spared them.

What Remains in the Shadows

They say the ghosts of Darr Mine are never silent.

At night along the river, you might hear the heavy tread of phantom boots, the hollow clang of spectral picks, or voices murmuring in Hungarian, Polish, Italian, and Greek—tongues of the dead.

Sometimes, the Sky Ferry glides across the black water, bearing the doomed in its creaking belly, their faces pale and flickering in spectral lamp-light.

These are men who never escaped the mine's hunger, and who walk forever in its shadow.

The Siren of the Loyalsock
(Wyoming County)

The haunting belongs to the Loyalsock, but because the creek feeds the Susquehanna—the same river that cuts through Wyoming County—the story bled into Wyoming County folklore through the shared waterways and lumber trade.

The Loyalsock Creek begins in the wilds that brush against western Wyoming County, its waters threading down into Sullivan and Lycoming Counties.

Along this waterway, lumbermen once poled rafts of timber south toward the Susquehanna. The river was their road, but also their grave.

One of the darkest stories told was of a girl named Cicely—sometimes called *Sweet Cicely*. She had lingered on a rocky ledge near the water, waiting for her lover, when a raftsman turned violent. In the struggle she was killed, her body left to the current and stone. The men who worked the Loyalsock swore she did not stay buried.

The Singing

Nights in the lumber camps pressed in like a suffocating fog. The men—tough from years of hard labor—grew wary when darkness crept along the water. It always began the same way: a woman's voice, so faint it seemed born from the mist itself, gliding over the black, restless current.

The song was sweet, but something in it was twisted, souring the air and knotting their insides with a fear that crawled beneath the skin. Some men clapped their hands to their ears, but the melody slithered through, impossible to block out. The unlucky ones found themselves humming it hours later, unable to recall when it had started.

Men saw her too. On storm-wracked nights, when the moon painted the world in bone-white light, a figure would appear on the ledge where Cicely had died. She wore a dress torn and sodden, hair tangled and trailing in the wind, her face pale as drowned porcelain. Her eyes— two hollow, gleaming pits—caught the moonlight but never blinked.

When rafts drifted near, the song swelled, impossibly loud. Some men, transfixed, found their hands loosening on the poles, their feet moving of their own accord. Logs splintered against the rocks as the river seized the rafts, dragging men down into the icy black. When their bodies surfaced days later, mouths gaping as if still trying to scream, the others whispered that Cicely had called them.

A Restless Current

The tales followed the Loyalsock as it wound downstream. Old-timers in Sullivan and Lycoming Counties whispered it; those farther north, in Wyoming County, spoke more cautiously. They knew the creek's headwaters, and they knew how a story flows like water—never bound by a county line.

Even when the haunting seemed to end—after another drowning was tied to her song—the name remained.

They called her the Siren of the Loyalsock.

Legacy

The legend does not belong to Wyoming County alone. But the Loyalsock begins there, its dark bends and fast channels rising from those hills. The people along its banks believed Cicely's spirit followed the current, her voice carrying with it—so that anywhere the creek flowed, the dead girl might be heard again.

So when the water is low and the night is still, stand on the bank and listen. If you're unlucky, you'll hear it: the thin, warbling melody of a dead girl, drifting just above the water.

Some say the song can slip inside you, filling your dreams with darkness.

Others warn that if you follow the music, you'll never be seen again.

The Hex Murder House
(York County)

Stewartstown, 1928

The old farmhouse of Nelson Rehmeyer squatted alone among the fields, a blackened husk against the November wind. Neighbors called him a powwower—one who healed with charms and words—but others whispered of curses spoken in the dark. They said his eyes could wither your luck, his touch could spoil the marrow in your bones, his very name poison the air if spoken after sundown.

John Blymire believed what he'd always heard in Stewartstown: that bad fortune could blacken a man's soul, and a powwower's grudge could damn you for generations. Misery haunted him—sickness, shadows moving in the corners, voices that spoke his name at midnight—until he was certain Rehmeyer had laid a hex.

With two others, he crept up to the farmhouse that bleak night, the ground brittle with frost, the silence suffocating. Inside, lantern shadows crawled like insects across the plaster as they demanded Rehmeyer's spell book, The Long Lost Friend.

He refused. What followed was butchery. They beat the old man until the rafters shook with his screams— sounds that crawled up through the fields and into the dreams of neighbors for years after. They bound him to the floorboards, the house suddenly thick with the stench of lamp oil and terror. When they struck a match and left his body to burn, the flames refused their work— devouring only flesh, leaving the timbers and stone untouched, as if even fire recoiled from the evil committed within those walls.

The Haunting

From that night on, the land soured. Cold seeped from the earth, and nothing grew right. Travelers whispered of a man drifting through the fields, broad-shouldered, his face half-ruined with burns, his eyes smoldering with something unholy. Windows glowed, though no lantern was lit. Some swore they heard guttural Pennsylvania Dutch curses in the wind, a chant that made dogs howl and children hide their faces.

At the threshold, the boards groan under invisible weight. A formless shadow slides past the window—watching, waiting, eyes burning in the night. The smell of scorched flesh clings to the walls, faint but undeniable when the hour is darkest.

They say Nelson Rehmeyer still wanders, his spirit restless, searching for the book never taken, for the life never finished. And in the dark, the echo of a fire that never burned enough flickers on his skin.

The Hex Murder House still stands. And they say if you walk too close, you'll hear him breathing in the walls.

The 7 Gates of Hell
(York County)

Trout Run Road—7 Gates of Hell *Urban Legend*
The Haunting Road

They whisper about Trout Run Road in Hellam Township, where the woods close in so tightly that night seems to fall even at noon. Hidden there are the Seven Gates of Hell—a scar on the land where, as one old-timer hissed, "Not even God will follow you past the third gate." Here, locals say, the living have crossed into damnation and never returned.

Origins in Fire

The legend begins with fire. Long ago, people claimed an insane asylum once stood deep in the timber. A blaze broke out one night, the flames roaring high into the black sky. Survivors recalled, "Their screams never stopped, not even after the roof caved in." Some inmates perished screaming, while others—wild-eyed and raving—escaped into the darkness of the trees. Panic swept the valley. To trap the wanderers, authorities—or in other tellings, a reclusive doctor—built a series of iron and stone gates. Seven in all.

Cursed Ground

But the prisoners were never caught. Instead, the road itself became cursed.

Travelers swore they saw phantoms stumbling along the brush, faces melted by firelight, chains clanking across the dirt.

As one terrified hunter told a reporter, "Something walked behind me all the way home, and it never had a face." The gates were said to draw the spirits, each one a threshold closer to damnation.

Those brave—or foolish—enough to wander beyond the first spoke of voices wailing in the branches and of unseen hands pulling them backward.

The Final Gate

And always, the tale ends the same: if you reach the seventh gate after midnight, the forest swallows you whole. "You never leave footprints past that last gate," warned a local, "because nothing comes back." The next step is not earth at all—but Hell.

Historical Note

For all its persistence, the legend bears scars of invention. No historical records confirm that a mental asylum ever existed on Trout Run Road. It is a timeworn urban legend, built on myth and exaggerated over time. That part appears to be embellishment layered onto an older tale. What does remain, however, are the gates themselves—real stone and metal barriers built by a local doctor in the 20th century. Over time, they became the skeleton on which rumor and horror hung their flesh.

Legacy of Fear

And still, on moonless nights, locals refuse to trespass beyond the first gate. Heed their caution—not only is the land private, but something restless lingers in those woods, indifferent to legend or law.

The Squonk
(Hemlock Forests throughout Pennsylvania)

The Hemlock Forests of Pennsylvania

No book of Pennsylvania legends is complete without mention of the state's most incredible and pitiable cryptid: *the Squonk.*

It wanders the hemlock forests at twilight, slinking through shadows, avoiding pools and ponds for fear of its own reflection.

So grotesque is its appearance that even it cannot bear the sight.

Each glimpse drives it to sob uncontrollably, its mournful cries drifting like a lament through the trees.

Its trail is marked not by footprints but by tears—dark, wet stains pressed into the earth. Even the most unskilled hunter could follow the sorrowful path. And yet, pursuit is hopeless. Frighten the Squonk, and it collapses into a trembling pool of tears, dissolving into nothing before human hands can touch it.

Hikers swear they have heard the sobs echoing through the hollows. But when they seek the source, they find only silence and the lingering damp of grief.

The Squonk does not fight, nor flee. It weeps—and then it vanishes.

More-Short Haunts

- **Logan Inn — New Hope, Bucks County**

Guests and employees describe apparitions, including a woman in white, along with unexplained scents and footsteps in one of the nation's oldest inns.

- **Jean Bonnet Tavern — Bedford, Bedford County**

Inn staff and diners have logged shadow figures, moving objects, and voices in this 18th-century tavern.

- **Hotel Bethlehem — Bethlehem, Northampton County**

The hotel openly chronicles resident spirits and reports from guests and employees.

- **Sachs Covered Bridge — Gettysburg, Adams County**

Night walkers report disembodied voices and footsteps on this historic bridge used during the battle

- **Cashtown Inn — Cashtown, Adams County**

Innkeepers and visitors report doors opening and the sound of troops; the inn was a Civil War staging point.

- **Farnsworth House Inn — Gettysburg, Adams County**

Staff speak of a child spirit "Mary" and soldier presences in a house pocked with battle scars.

- **Pennsylvania Hall, Gettysburg College — Gettysburg, Adams County**

Multiple campus sources repeat the elevator story—riders opening the doors to a ghostly wartime hospital scene before the car returned.

- **Powel House — Philadelphia, Philadelphia County**

Caretakers and guests have reported colonial-era figures and marching soldiers tied to the Revolutionary War lore inside this 18th-century mansion-museum.

- **Betsy Ross House — Philadelphia, Philadelphia County**
Staff and visitors have reported weeping sounds and a shadowed female figure during evening programs at the Old City museum.

- **USS Olympia (Independence Seaport Museum) — Philadelphia, Philadelphia County**
Museum staff and investigators cite footsteps and voices aboard the Spanish–American War cruiser during sanctioned after-hours events.

- **Hill View Manor — New Castle, Lawrence County**
Former poor farm/nursing home where staff and tour groups document shadow figures, disembodied voices, and repeated visual anomalies.

- **Hotel Conneaut — Conneaut Lake, Crawford County**
Guests and employees report a bride named "Elizabeth," cold spots, and apparitions near the ballroom and lakeside corridors.

- **Baker Mansion — Altoona, Blair County**
Docents and visitors report music, moving objects, and a watching presence linked to the Baker family legends.

- **Fort Hunter Mansion — Harrisburg, Dauphin County**
Staff and investigators have logged knocks, footsteps, and voices during controlled investigations in the 19th-century rooms.

- **Pennhurst State School — Spring City, Chester County**
Former institution where security and investigators document voices and figures in multiple buildings during regulated access.

- **Pittsburgh Playhouse (Point Park University) — Pittsburgh, Allegheny County**
Faculty and students have long reported a "Lady in White," stage whispers, and door activity after hours.

- **Kennywood Park — West Mifflin, Allegheny County**
Park employees trade stories about a boy near the lagoon and other after-hours apparitions around famous rides.
- **Sun Inn — Bethlehem, Northampton County**
Staff accounts include a woman in period dress and movement in locked rooms at this colonial-era inn.
- **Moravian Book Shop — Bethlehem, Northampton County**
Books shifting, footsteps, and disembodied voices have been reported by employees in America's oldest bookstore.
- **Graeme Park (Keith House) — Horsham, Montgomery County**
Interpreters and visitors cite recurring experiences associated with Elizabeth Graeme Fergusson and other presences.
- **Van Sant Covered Bridge — Solebury Township, Bucks County**
Night visitors report sudden temperature drops and a figure seen at mid-span.
- **Brinton Lodge — Douglassville, Berks County**
Guests and former owners reported laughter, voices, and a "ghost party" in the old music room
- **Yuengling Brewery — Pottsville, Schuylkill County**
Staff tours recount shadow figures and voices in the 19th-century lagering tunnels beneath the brewery.
- **Laurel Hill Cemetery — Philadelphia, Philadelphia County** Caretakers and guides have collected long-running reports of voices and figures among the historic monuments.
- **Black Bass Hotel — Lumberville, Bucks County**
Owners and patrons describe a well-dressed gentleman and poltergeist-like activity in a riverside landmark dating to the 1700s.

- **Penn Wells Hotel — Wellsboro, Tioga County**

Guests report lights and doors acting on their own and a woman in antique dress along the halls.

- **Hotel Wayne — Honesdale, Wayne County**

Employees and overnight guests share reports of apparitions and knocks through this 19th-century hostelry.

- **Struthers Library Theatre — Warren, Warren County**

Performers report footsteps and a male figure watching from the balcony during rehearsals.

- **Palace Theatre — Greensburg, Westmoreland County**

Technicians and staff note cold spots, whispers, and a woman near the box seats after hours.

- **Bushy Run Battlefield — Jeannette/Harrison City, Westmoreland County**

Reenactors and staff report marching sounds and soldier figures on dusk trails at the 1763 battle site.

- **Dickinson College ("Old West") — Carlisle, Cumberland County**

Students and faculty have shared decades of accounts of a woman and child in the stairwells and auditorium corridors.

- **Presque Isle Lighthouse — Erie, Erie County**

Docents and visiting teams cite footsteps on the stairs and a figure at the lantern room during special events.

- **Haldeman Mansion — Bainbridge, Lancaster County**

Volunteers report piano music, voices, and a woman at the windows of the riverfront mansion.

- **Penn State: Schwab Auditorium & Old Botany — State College, Centre County**

University features compile student/staff reports tied to Frances Atherton and other campus apparitions.

- **Bedford Springs Resort — Bedford, Bedford County**

Employees and guests have reported a woman in white and door activity in older wings after restoration.

- **Grand Midway Hotel — Windber, Somerset County**

Owners and visitors document frequent activity—voices, moving objects, and full-figure sightings—in the famously haunted hotel.

- **Railroad House Inn — Marietta, Lancaster County**

Management logs persistent reports of footsteps, knocks, and a female figure in historic rooms.

- **Nemacolin Castle (Bowman House) — Brownsville, Fayette County**

Docents and investigators have recorded voices and apparitions in the riverside landmark.

- **Brandywine Battlefield Area — Chadds Ford,**

Guides and locals circulate accounts of marching sounds and soldier figures on foggy nights in and around the preserved fields. Lies mostly in Delaware County, though the battle also touched Chester County.

- **Radisson Lackawanna Station Hotel — Scranton, Lackawanna County**

Hotel staff and guests report a woman in old-fashioned clothing and footsteps in empty corridors.

- **Scranton Cultural Center (Masonic Temple) — Scranton, Lackawanna County**

Stage crews and tour leaders recount balcony shadows and voices backstage in the 1930 landmark.

- **Shawnee Inn & Golf Resort — Shawnee-on-Delaware, Monroe County**

Guests and employees describe apparitions and piano music with no player in the historic resort.

- **King George II Inn — Bristol, Bucks County**

Owners and patrons openly talk about a top-hat gentleman and moving objects among recurring reports in the colonial tavern.

- **Warner Theatre — Erie, Erie County**

Theatre staff permitted a documented overnight investigation after years of claims about a woman seen on the balcony stairs.

- **Harmony Inn — Harmony/Zelienople, Butler County**

North Country Brewing staff and diners have reported footsteps, voices, and multiple apparitions in the restored 19th-century inn.

- **Physick House — Philadelphia, Philadelphia County**

Tour guides and visitors tell of strange footsteps and presences in the former home of Dr. Philip Syng Physick.

- **Jennie Wade House – Gettysburg, Adams County**

Visitors and staff claim to hear footsteps, whispers, and the sound of crying in the home where Jennie Wade was killed by a stray bullet in July 1863.

- **Mishler Theatre – Altoona, Blair County**

Actors and staff report a spectral figure in the balcony and unexplained music in the historic 1906 playhouse.

- **Albright Memorial Library – Scranton, Lackawanna County**

Staff report books moving on their own and a woman in Victorian dress walking the upper floors.

- **Baleroy Mansion – Chestnut Hill, Philadelphia**

Known as "the most haunted house in America," visitors have described a cursed blue chair and a hostile spirit nicknamed Amanda.

- **General Wayne Inn – Merion, Montgomery County**

Dating to 1704, it has reports of Hessian soldier ghosts, strange reflections, and unexplained apparitions in mirrors.

- **Fort Mifflin — Philadelphia, Philadelphia County**

Staff docents and visitors report a "Screaming Woman," phantom soldiers, and footsteps in casemates at this Revolutionary War fort, which regularly hosts paranormal programs.

- **Albright Mansion / The Haunting of Jim Thorpe (Carbon County)**

The Asa Packer Mansion is better known historically, but Jim Thorpe (formerly Mauch Chunk) has several tied ghost legends that are very well-publicized in tours.

- **Dobbin House Tavern** (Adams County)

Popular haunted restaurant.

- **Devil's Den (Gettysburg Battlefield)** – One of the most cited battlefield ghost spots.

- **Byberry State Hospital (Philadelphia, Philadelphia County)**

  Though demolished, this infamous asylum was a hotspot of urban legend and paranormal stories.

Citations

Jenny Wade: (39.823330, -77.230646) Little Book of Gettysburg Ghosts, Quackenbush, Jannette

Jacob Hummelbaugh Farm (39.807943, -77.231564) Little Book of Gettysburg Ghosts, Quackenbush, Jannette

Martha Grinder: (Three Rivers Heritage Trail: Three Rivers Heritage **Trail** 40.447850, -80.000055) "The American Borgia: Execution of Martha Grinder," New York
Times, January 20, 1866, p. 8.

Dead Man Hollow—(40.317985, -79.840733)Pittsburgh Post-Gazette Pittsburgh, Pennsylvania Thursday,
April 06, 2000 - Page 117
Pittsburgh Daily Post Pittsburgh, Pennsylvania August 03,

Chickasaw Mine: Private: (40.954431, -79.457924) The Philadelphia Inquirer Philadelphia, Pennsylvania Mar 10, 1913
geocaching.com/geocache/GC3KK8X

Ghost Dog:
bcpahistory.org/beavercounty/BeaverCountyTopical/ghostsandphenonmena/GhostofRaccoonCreek.html

Summitt Cut Bridge (40.816569, -80.374853)
hauntedplaces.org/item/summit-cut-bridge

Black Dog: paoddities.blogspot.com/2021/01/the-ghost-dog-of-woodbury-and-mystery.html
Altoona Tribune. March 26, 1923

Blue-Eyed Six:
Murder by Gaslight —
"The Blue-Eyed Six" murderbygaslight.com/2011/10/blue-eyed-six.html
"The Blue-Eyed Six" by John T. McWilliams, Pennsylvania Heritage

Lost Children: Lost Children of the Alleghenies Monument Imler, PA 16655 (40.296534, -78.603747)
Bedford Gazette Bedford, Pennsylvania May 11, 1906

Returned Coin: Canton *Ohio Repository, Friday July 9, 1819 Remarkable Instance of Delusion*

Adaline Bavor: *Irish Creek Bridge (40.459051, -75.979759)*
Grave: Bellemans Church Cemetery Mohrsville, Berks County, Pennsylvania (40.4590028,-76.0310528) Plot Old Cemetery, Row 3 #49
"The Murder of Adaline Bavor," Erie Observer, Erie, Pa., 14 November, 1857, Page 4
Reading Times Reading, Pennsylvania Thu, May 30, 1889 Page 1
"The Murder of Miss Bavor," *The Compiler,* Gettysburg, Pa., Monday, 3 May, 1858, Page 2.
"A Clue," *The Compiler,* Gettysburg, Pa., Monday, 3 May, 1858, Page 1.

Schaumboch's Tavern: (40.633520, -75.980427)
hagenbuch.org/schambachers-tavern-real-ghost-story/
The Specter of Alexander Hutchinson:
genealogytrails.com/penn/blair/news_crime.html
Lewistown Gazette Lewistown, Pennsylvania Sep 20, 1850 Page 2
Horseshoe Curve:
discoverypa.blogspot.com/2014/10/the-legend-of-horseshoe-curve-tunnel.html
hauntsandhistory.blogspot.com/2009/05/spooks-of-curve.html
Altoona Mirror Altoona, Pennsylvania
Wilkes-Barre Times Leader, the Evening News Wilkes-Barre, Pennsylvania
Dec 31, 1909
The Daily Courier Connellsville, Pennsylvania Feb 18, 1947
Pennsylvania Railroad's Red Arrow Derailment:
centralpahistory.blogspot.com/2021/02/the-red-arrow-wreck-blair-county.html
White Lady of Wopsy:
Pennsylvania Ghosts and Legends by Charles J. Adams III
Barclay:
Elmira Advertiser dated February 8, 1882
sites.rootsweb.com/~pasulliv/SullivanCountyHistoricalSociety/Barclay.htm
occult-world.com/barclay-cemetery/
Doans Cave:
doangang.org/maps/bucks-county-caves-map/
alltrails.com/trail/us/pennsylvania/doans-cave Parking: (40.43446, -75.09758)
(cave: 40.43483, -75.09403)
Red eyes:
Conrad Snyder Cemetery: (40.97670, -80.00460)
youtube.com/watch?v=hdbDACLjrh0
findagrave.com/memorial/18543326/conrad-snyder
Rolling Hills Coal Mine:
lhhv.org/local-folk-lore/
Beil Hill Road
1-59 Township Rd 542 Greenville, PA 16125 (41.348733, -80.350289)
The Record-Argus Greenville, Pennsylvania Oct 30, 1971 Page 12 Legend of
the Lady and the Lantern
Puppet Man:
Altoona Tribune Altoona, Pennsylvania • , Nov 7, 1941 Page 6
Molly Maguires: Old Jail Museum (Carbon County Jail)
Address: 128 W Broadway, Jim Thorpe, PA 18229
GPS Coordinates: 40.86371, -75.73288

This is the original 1871 jail where several Molly Maguires were imprisoned and executed. The famous handprint of Alexander Campbell is still visible in Cell 17 and can be seen on guided tours.

Kenny, Kevin. *Making Sense of the Molly Maguires*. Oxford University Press, 1998.

A scholarly and detailed account that examines the social, political, and labor context of the Mollies, and challenges the narrative of them as a unified terror group.

Aurand, A. Monroe. *The Mollie Maguires: The True Story of Labor Violence in the Coal Fields*. The Aurand Press, 1940.

McParland, James. *Pinkerton Detective Reports* (1870s) Original testimony and reports from the Pinkerton agent who infiltrated the Mollies. Portions reprinted in historical trial documents.

Scotia Black Ghost:

Source: Williams, Harry M. *The Story of Scotia*. State College: Centre County Historical Society, 1992.

Bert Delige was buried on a plot of ground owned by the Delige family not quite 100 yards from the house.

(40.801630, -77.952990)

The Giant Ghost of Brush Valley and Other . . .Centre Daily Times State College, Pennsylvania · Saturday, October 28, 2006

Centre Daily Times State College, Pennsylvania · Sat, Oct 31, 1981 Page 1 .findagrave.com/cemetery/2721888/bert-delige-burial-site

Paoli Battlefield:

Paoli Battlefield Historical Park Monument Ave &, Wayne Ave, Malvern, PA 19355 (40.030384, -75.515770)

battlefields.org/learn/head-tilting-history/haunting-encounters-revolutionary-ghouls

Twin Tunnels:

countylinesmagazine.com/article/chester-countys-scary-stories-and-haunted-tours

Valley Creek Road Downingtown, PA 19335 (40.004734, -75.665614)

Crybaby Cemetery:

1099-901 T-384 Knox, PA 16232 (41.206878, -79.576889)

pawilds.com/ghosts-pa-wilds-haunted-cemeteries-cook-forest

frightfind.com/most-haunted-cemeteries-in-america

"Haunted Clarion – Part Two: 'Crybaby Cemetery'" Published by ExploreClarion.com on October 23, 2021

Clearfield Jail:

300 N 2nd St, Clearfield, PA 16830 (41.025885, -78.438470)

wjactv.com/news/local/paranormal-investigation-team-explores-former-clearfield-county-jail

Clinton:

Pine-Loganton Rd (41.112120, -77.306299)

Shoemaker, Henry W. More Pennsylvania Mountain Stories. Altoona, PA: Altoona Tribune Publishing Company, 1912. pp. 185–187.

Maynard, D. S. (2023). Historical view of Clinton County.

Bloody 32 and Ghost Plane:

thepennsylvaniarambler.wordpress.com

Swatera Ghosts: Fiddlers Elbow Rd Hummelstown, PA 17036 (40.256257, -76.731671)

Harrisburg Telegraph Harrisburg, Pennsylvania Sat, Jun 3, 1882 Page 5

Ghost of Elizabeth "Harriot" Wilson

Ghost stories linger—babies crying near the site of their murder (now near Regal Cinemas in Edgmont), a phantom horseman passing the old jail or gallows, William's footsteps and sobs in the caverns, and most often, a woman drifting along West Chester Pike and through the surrounding woods, searching.

Ashmead, Henry Graham & William Shaler Johnson (1883). Historical Sketch of Chester on Delaware. Chester PA: Republican Steam Printing.

Teeters, Negley (1967). "...Hang By the Neck...". Springfield, IL: Charles Thomas.

facebook.com/groups/204870274130594

Betty Knox:

Quackenbush, J. (2020). Pennsylvania ghosts and haunts: West Pennsylvania.

Along Dunbar Creek Betty Knox Road Dunbar, Pennsylvania 15431 (39.944499, -79.581229)

The Morning Herald Wed Feb 25,1925

The_Pittsburgh Press Jun 3,1923

Quackenbush, J. (2020). Pennsylvania ghosts and haunts: West Pennsylvania.

Stove Pipe:

Quackenbush, J. (2020). Pennsylvania ghosts and haunts: West Pennsylvania.

Rices Landing, PA 15357 (39.948680, -80.003947)

—Venable, W. (n.d.). Retired Professor Recounts History of Rices Landing: uppermon.org/news/

Other/OR-Rices_Landing-2Feb12.html

Shades of Death:

Intersection of Bethel Ridge Road and Shades of Death Road Avella, PA 15312 (40.314967, -80.490149)

To Intersection of Shades of Death Road and Campbell Drive Avella, PA 15312 (40.306545, -80.465302)

Observer-Reporter, "What's in a Name? Rumors Swirl Around Shades of Death Road" (June 23, 2025)

The New York Times, July 18, 1922

Crow Rock Massacre:
Crow Rock Massacre Site Crow Rock Road Wind Ridge, PA 15380 (39.927666, -80.505720)
Quackenbush, J. (2020). Pennsylvania ghosts and haunts: West Pennsylvania.
facebook.com+3theclio.com+3visitgreene.org+3visitgreene.org
Janesville Pike:
PA-453 Tyrone, PA 16686 (40.706282, -78.31164)
Elk County Jail — Ridgway, PA (Elk County)
300 Center Street, Ridgway, Pennsylvania (41.421059, -78.727823)
Minster Creek and Hickory Creek:
Allegheny National Forest - Minister Creek Trail Clarendon, PA 16313 (41.635466, -79.16686)
Hickory Creek Wilderness Trail State Rte 2002, Tidioute, PA 16351 (41.698902, -79.252976)
The Tionesta Recorder and Forest Press
Online Forums and Hiker Reports-Hiking forums (e.g., Trail Journals, Reddit r/PennsylvaniaHiking)
"Ghosts of the Allegheny National Forest," *Pennsylvania Legends & Lore*
Dykeman Park:
121-199 W. Dykeman Road Shippensburg, PA 17257
Shippensburg Borough – Dykeman Park Information
Shippensburg Borough: Parks & Recreation
Franklin County Visitors Bureau – Haunted Franklin County
Franklin County Fright Sites (Tour Listings & Local Publications)
The Sentinel (cumberlink.com) and Shippensburg News-Chronicle
Death Curve:
paoddities.blogspot.com/2023/10/the-headless-ghost-of-waynesboro.html
Waynesboro Press Nov. 27, 1920
Sideling Tunnel:
 Parking/Trailhead: Pike 2 Bike Lot— 3300-3346 Pump Station Road Waterfall, Pennsylvania 16689
(40.048771, -78.095859)
Quackenbush, J. (2023). Haunted hikes of the Appalachian hills & hollers 2: Hiking trails with legends, ghost stories, and abandoned places.
Phantom Stagecoach of Punxsutawney Pike:
2400-2686 Pike Rd Punxsutawney, PA 15767 (40.993346, -78.849338)
Thomas White's *Ghosts of Southwestern Pennsylvania*
Silver Mines:
Oroblanco, "Legends of Lost Silver Mines in Pennsylvania," Jan. 19, 2012
Licking Creek:
Licking Creek Rd Milford Township, PA (40.533473, -77.55463)
Licking Creek, Juniata County, U.S. Geological Survey; *Keystone Canoeing*, Edward Gertler, 2004

Local column, *Lewistown Sentinel*, "Ghosts, hauntings and witches, oh my!", Oct 30, 2021

Fulton Opera House:
12 North Prince Street, Lancaster, PA 17603 (40.038105, -76.308186)
Pennsylvania Gazette, December 1763.
Dixon, David. Never Come to Peace Again: Pontiac's Uprising and the Fate of the British Empire in North America. University of Oklahoma Press, 2005
LancasterOnline, "Ghostly tales haunt historic Fulton Opera House," October 28, 2015.
lancasteronline.com/features/ghostly-tales-haunt-historic-fulton-opera-house/article_46e1d3b2-7d8e-11e5-9d3e-ab9efad6cc52.html
WGAL News 8, "Haunted History: The Fulton Theatre's Ghost Stories," October 31, 2017.
wgal.com/article/haunted-history-fulton-theatre-ghost-stories/13123633
Intelligencer Journal/Lancaster New Era, "Fulton Theatre offers haunted tours," October 22, 2009.
Martin, Tim. "Lancaster's Fulton Theatre: Haunted by History," Paranormal Pennsylvania, 2014.
Brubaker, Jack. "The Scribbler: Ghosts at the Fulton Opera House?" LancasterOnline, October 2012.

Chickies Rock:
Chickies Rock County Park, Columbia, PA 17512 (40.061356, -76.516843)

Historic McConnell's Mill Covered Bridge:
McConnells Mill Rd, Portersville, PA 16051 (40.953083, -80.170299)

Union Canal Tunnel:
25th Street & Union Canal Drive Lebanon, PA 17046 (40.349049, -76.460789)

Saylor Cement Kilns:
Coplay Cement Company Kilns (Saylor Park Industrial Museum), 299 N 2nd St, Hokendauqua, PA 18052
Online Forums & Community Posts
Reddit – r/ghosts, r/LehighValley:
Posts and comments from local urban explorers and ghost enthusiasts describe personal experiences at the kilns, including shadow sightings and unexplained chills.
Reddit - r/ghosts: "Creepiest place in the Lehigh Valley?"
Facebook Groups: Local groups like "Lehigh Valley Paranormal" and "Lehigh Valley History" frequently feature user-shared photos, ghost anecdotes, and debates about haunted sites, including the Saylor Kilns.
Blogs & Articles Lehigh Valley Haunts (blog):
Only in Your State – Pennsylvania:
The Morning Call (Allentown):
Ghost Tours & Oral Tradition- Lehigh Valley ghost tours
"Patchtown" Catherine and the Burning Mines:

The Citizens' Voice, September 7, 2015: "Laurel Run's fire, 100 years later"
Pennsylvania Department of Environmental Protection: "Laurel Run Mine Fire"
Laurel Run: A Centennial History by John R. Prokopchak (1982)
Ghosts of the Wyoming Valley by Charles J. Adams III (Schiffer Publishing, 2014)

Ralston Ghosts:
Ghosts of the West Branch Valley by Thomas White (Arcadia Publishing, 2010)
Williamsport Sun-Gazette (Local Newspaper)
Local Histories & Rail Heritage Groups

Kinzua Bridge:
The Kinzua Bridge was originally built in 1882 as a railroad viaduct and, after a partial collapse in 2003 due to a tornado, now serves as a scenic Skywalk and historical landmark.
Kinzua Bridge State Park 96 Viaduct Road, Mount Jewett, PA 16740 (41.759000, -78.586000)
Nearest Town: Mount Jewett (about 5 miles southeast)
Region: Pennsylvania Wilds, north of the Allegheny National Forest

Cotters Hole:
lewistownsentinel.com/opinion/local-columns/2021/10/ghosts-hauntings-and-witches-oh-my/
facebook.com/mifflincountyhistoricalsociety/posts/the-legend-of-cotters-hole-is-a-ghost-story-set-in-the-juniata-river-valley-wher/1021708184516102/

Valley Forge:
Valley Forge National Historical Park 1400 N Outer Line Dr, King of Prussia, PA 19406 (40.099898, -75.446145)
Waldo, Albigence. The Diary of Dr. Albigence Waldo, Surgeon at Valley Forge, 1777-1778.
Martin, Joseph Plumb. A Narrative of a Revolutionary Soldier: Some of the Adventures, Dangers, and Sufferings of Joseph Plumb Martin.
Adams, Charles J. III. Ghost Stories of Valley Forge and Phoenixville.
Valley Forge National Historical Park – Official Website:
NPS – Ghosts of Valley Forge

Katy's Church:
northcentralpa.com/life/the-haunted-legend-of-katys-church-in-millville/article_6639356c-35fa-11ec-a08f-9b7897dc24c7.html

Hexenkopf:
Hexenkopf Hill is located in Williams Township, Northampton County, Pennsylvania. (40.621893, -75.243040)
Heindel, Ned D. Hexenkopf: History, Healing & Hexerei. Easton, PA: Northampton County Historical and Genealogical Society, 2nd ed, 2002.
Henry, M.S. History of the Lehigh Valley. Easton, PA: Bixler and Corwin, 1860

Wagoneer's Gap:
The gap is traversed by **Waggoner's Gap Road (PA Route 74)**.
It is located **about 10 miles north of Carlisle, PA**, and just south of the Perry County line. Address for Hawk Watch parking: Waggoner's Gap Hawk Watch Waggoner's Gap Rd Carlisle, PA 17013 (40.278634, -77.276310)

Washington Square:
Christopher, Thomas. "Haunted Philadelphia: Washington Square." Visit Philadelphia. visitphilly.com/articles/philadelphia/haunted-philadelphia/
McMahon, Patrick. "Ghosts of Washington Square." Hidden City Philadelphia. hiddencityphila.org/2014/10/the-ghosts-of-washington-square/

Eastern State Pen:
Dickens, Charles. American Notes for General Circulation (1842).
Philadelphia Inquirer, Feb. 1930 (Capone disturbed in his cell).
Oral accounts preserved by Eastern State Penitentiary Historic Site (Joseph Taylor, 1990s).
Philadelphia Daily News, 1970s–80s Halloween feature reports on paranormal activity.
Paul Kahan, Eastern State Penitentiary: A History (2008).

Shohola Train Wreck:
Wreck happened at a spot known as "King and Fuller's Cut," approximately one mile west of the Shohola railroad station. Today, the exact location is somewhat remote, with the original tracks long gone, but the general area is along what is now Shohola Township, near Route 6 and close to Shohola Creek. Shohola Railroad Historical Marker Route 434 (Shohola Township), near the bridge over the Shohola Creek
Shohola, PA 18458
PAPI Paranormal Investigators Quote: The PAPI (Paranormal and Psychic Investigations) group conducted an investigation at the Shohola Train Wreck site.
Quote from a visitor comment on the Shohola Train Wreck Monument page on Find a Grave
Shohola Civil War Train Wreck – Historical Marker Database
Shohola Township Official Website
Find a Grave: Shohola Train Wreck Memorial

Ghost of Austin:
Austin, PA: A small borough in southern Potter County, historically known for its lumber industry and the tragic Austin Dam flood.
Lou Bernard, "The Ghost of Amandon Baker," in The PA Wilds Are Calling: Ghost Stories of Northcentral Pennsylvania, PA Wilds Center for Entrepreneurship, 2018. PA Wilds Blog Archive
"Ghosts of the Lumber Camps," Potter County Historical Society Newsletter, Vol. 22, No. 3, Fall 2007.

Haunted Pennsylvania: Ghosts and Strange Phenomena of the Keystone State by Mark Nesbitt, Stackpole Books, 2006

Breaker Boys:

Thomas White, "Ghosts of the Pennsylvania Anthracite Coal Region" (History Press, 2013), pp. 42–44.

David DeKok, "Fire Underground: The Ongoing Tragedy of the Centralia Mine Fire" (Globe Pequot, 1986)

Schuylkill County Historical Society archives: Oral histories and local tours referencing the breaker boy hauntings

Penns Creek Massacre Ghosts:

The Pennsylvania Center for the Book, Penns Creek Massacre

Charles McCool Snyder, Union County, Pennsylvania: A Celebration of History, 2000

The Pennsylvania Gazette, October 30, 1755.

The Pennsylvania Gazette, November 20, 1755

Glades Pike:

Thomas White, Haunted Roads of Western Pennsylvania, The History Press, 2014, pp. 110-113.

Trackwalker:

Henry W. Shoemaker, Susquehanna Legends (1913).

Haunted Vista:

Anna S. Mine

atlasobscura.com/places/haunted-vista

Legend of White Deer Pike:

The earliest printed versions appear in Henry W. Shoemaker's folklore collections in the early 1900s.

Pennsylvania Mountain Stories (1907)

North Pennsylvania Minstrelsy (1919)

The Ghostly Grave of Allen Ketlaw

"Old Time Tales of Warren County" by Arch Bristow

pawilds.com/ghosts-of-the-pa-wilds-the-ghostly-grave-of-allen-ketlaw/

Hex House:

Hanna, Sara. "The Hex Murder: Pennsylvania's Most Famous Witchcraft Trial." Pennsylvania Heritage, Summer 2003.

www.ingramcontent.com/pod-product-compliance
Lightning Source LLC
Chambersburg PA
CBHW070834280626
47161CB00015B/592